LUCKY NUMBER THIRTEEN
A THREE RIVERS RANCH ROMANCE BOOK 10

LIZ ISAACSON

AEJ
CREATIVE WORKS

Copyright © 2020 by Elana Johnson, writing as Liz Isaacson

All rights reserved.

No part of this book may be reproduced in any form or by any electronic or mechanical means, including information storage and retrieval systems, without written permission from the author, except for the use of brief quotations in a book review.

ISBN-13: 978-1-953506-16-0

SCRIPTURE

"I will freely sacrifice unto thee: I will praise thy name, O Lord; for it is good."

PSALMS 54:6

CHAPTER ONE

"Tanner!"

Tanner Wolf turned at the sound of his name in a female voice. A blond man strode toward him, his hand secured in a dark haired woman's.

A smile warmed his soul. "Brynn."

She laughed as he embraced her, and Ethan's grin seemed as wide as the sky over Montana. "Hey, Tanner." He slapped Tanner on the back. "That was some impressive roping."

"Thanks." He brushed some invisible dust from his hands and a lot of very visible dirt from his chaps. "Nothin' like me and you, but Dallas does all right."

"All right?" Brynn scoffed. "You'll take first with that, and from what I hear, you guys won't be beat this year."

Tanner tried to shrug off their compliments. Since Ethan had chosen Brynn over rodeo, chosen Three Rivers over Colorado, chosen his faith over everything, Tanner

1

had searched his soul. It wasn't easy, and he'd found a lot of darkness inside. He still wasn't all the way where he wanted to be, and being humble didn't come naturally to him.

After all, he'd spent the last thirty years of his life trying to be the best and celebrating when he was.

"You're comin' out to the ranch for the picnic, right?" Ethan asked. Tanner had been in touch with him over the past couple of years, and when his manager had added the Three Rivers rodeo to his schedule, Tanner had called Ethan first.

"Yeah, of course. Tomorrow at four. I've been to the ranch before."

"You haven't seen my training facilities," Brynn said as a group of cowgirls walked by. Her gaze followed them, and Tanner wondered if she missed the rodeo circuit. She'd quit and never looked back, but a glint rode in her eye that Tanner recognized.

"I'll come early," Tanner said. "Will you guys be out there?"

"We can go out whenever we want," Brynn said.

"I want to see your place too," Tanner said. "Ethan's been bragging about how he built it from the ground up."

"I haven't been bragging."

"I believe you said, 'with my bare hands, Tanner. I built a whole house with my bare hands.'"

Ethan chuckled, and a wave of gratitude washed over Tanner. He couldn't believe Ethan's forgiveness had come so quickly, had healed him so completely. But it had done both, and though he'd never told Ethan, it was his forgiveness that had set Tanner down the path toward a relationship with God.

Of course, that had meant his relationships with women had cooled considerably as he navigated his way toward becoming the kind of man he wanted to be. In fact, his last date had been over a year ago, and that relationship had fizzled before the end of the evening.

"Mister Wolf, you're up in twenty," a rodeo volunteer said, stepping into their conversation.

Tanner took a deep breath, his nerves blossoming into a hill of ants. "All right, wish me luck."

"Who'd you draw?" Ethan asked.

"Lucky Number Thirteen," Tanner said, his voice a note higher than normal. "I've never ridden him to the bell."

Brynn's dark eyes caught on his and her hand landed on his forearm. "You'll get 'im this time." She added a smile to her statement, and Tanner couldn't detect a hint of falseness in her voice.

He managed to smile, mash his cowboy hat further down on his head, and follow the volunteer to the loading chutes.

He'd ridden hundreds of bulls over his twelve-year career. He'd drawn easy wins and nasty animals. He'd never had a bull he hadn't been able to ride. Eventually, they all succumbed to Tanner and the eight-second bell.

He eyed Lucky Number Thirteen, the black and white bull he'd come up against in San Antonio earlier this year.

He'd only made it three seconds on the animal, and that disastrous ride played through his mind as the other riders took their turns.

Finally, he sat on the bull's back. He pulled the rope across his palm tight, tight. He drew breath after breath to calm his heart, relax his muscles. None of the calming techniques worked, and he had a brief second to wonder if he should've asked for a helmet before the bell rang and the gate opened.

The crowd blurred as it always did while he rode. He only felt the bull's muscles beneath his body. Only listened for the alarm signaling he'd made it to eight seconds. Only breathed once the ride ended.

Lucky Number Thirteen reared, driving right back into Tanner's chest. He slipped, and he knew he was going off despite his strong muscles and iron will trying to hold him on the bull's back.

His feet didn't hit the dirt first; his back did. Hard. The air in his lungs seized, and he couldn't take another breath. The bright lights in the arena went dark as the bull kicked, loomed above him, and all Tanner saw was dark sky and dark animal flesh, and a horrifying dark hoof as it crashed into his ribs.

He instinctively curled into himself, protecting his most vital organs. Around him, he heard shouts, silence, the announcers, the snuffling of the bull, the call of the clowns. He couldn't breathe, couldn't breathe, and pressed his chin to his chest and kept his elbows up as another lightning hot pain shot through his back, down into both his legs.

Time seemed to slow and everything felt shrouded in darkness.

Finally, everything brightened again, and Tanner relaxed. His brain seemed to be working just fine, but every cell in his body screamed in pain. He groaned as he started to uncurl.

"Don't move," someone said, his hand landing lightly on Tanner's forehead. He said something else, his gaze darting away, but Tanner closed his eyes and focused on breathing. Breathing was good. Breathing was necessary.

Movement happened around him. Men spoke in calm voices. Tanner felt the summer air turn cold as something pooled beneath his head. He tried to reach for it, but someone stopped him.

"Lie still, Tanner." A familiar face, with bright green eyes and that shock of blond hair, filled his vision.

"Ethan," Tanner moaned. *Help me,* he prayed, and though he was new to the whole communicating with God idea, the thought felt natural.

"You're fine, cowboy." Ethan's eyes said otherwise, and Tanner tried to focus on them. But they turned lighter and lighter, going into seafoam and mint before they faded into whiteness.

"Stay with me," Ethan commanded, but Tanner couldn't. He closed his eyes against the pain and let unconsciousness take him somewhere where he wasn't lying in his own blood in the middle of the rodeo arena.

When he woke, a pair of eyes the color of the ocean blinked at him. "There you are, Mister Wolf." The woman spoke in a slow cadence, her accent Texan and sweet. She glanced down at his chart, wrote something, and looked at him again. "How are you feeling?"

He couldn't vocalize the words he used to, and his back and arm muscles seemed to have forgotten how to shrug.

"My name's Summer, and I'll be your nurse today. Now Jean said you slept all night, and came through your surgery just fine."

He blinked at her, a searing pain in his throat. He could only think, *Surgery?*

"Now, you'll have to get up in a few hours and take a walk around." She grinned at him, and he thought she had the most wonderful pink lips, the most beautiful white teeth. His first instinct was to smile back, and he tried, but something seemed to be wrong with his mouth.

"I don't want any complaints when I come back," she said, her eyes dipping to his lips. "I'll go get Margie, and we'll get that tube out of your throat." She disappeared from his line of sight, and Tanner found pain in every part of his body. How Summer thought he could answer her questions with a tube down his throat, he didn't know.

She returned lickety split, and before he knew it, the two nurses had removed the tube from his throat.

"He's making urine," the other nurse said. She beamed

at him, and he'd never been prouder of his body for functioning the way it should. She was closer to his mother's age, and panic pounded through him.

"My...mom?" His throat hurt, and Summer was there, holding out a glass of water. He gulped it greedily as Margie explained that she'd been notified and that she should be here soon.

"There's a couple of friends out in the waiting room," she said. "Should I send them in?"

"How much pain are you in?" Summer asked before Tanner could answer Margie.

"Is 'about to die' on your chart?" he croaked.

She grinned. "Yes, we call that a ten. I'll bring you something."

"A lot of something," he said as a pain in his leg fired on all cylinders. "Something strong."

Margie met Summer's eye and the two nurses exchanged a glance. "Something strong, Mister Wolf," Summer said, her voice full of fun and flirtation.

Tanner sat back in bed as they left, warning himself to maintain distance from Summer. He didn't live in Three Rivers, and she'd go home—maybe to a husband and a family—later that day.

She sure is pretty though, he thought as he waited for his medicine and his friends. The friends came first, and Ethan and Brynn looked like they hadn't gone home to sleep.

Tears tracked down Brynn's cheeks as she leaned over

and gave Tanner a light hug. He couldn't help the groan of pain from the movement and she jerked back. "Sorry."

"I'm fine." He pushed himself up in bed, a flash of discomfort spreading through his right leg. "Aren't I fine, Ethan?"

He watched his friend for the signs he needed. Ethan kept his face a blank slate, but the intensity of his swallow told Tanner everything.

"Yeah," Ethan said. "You're going to be just fine, Tanner."

Tanner looked away as emotion surged up his throat. He knew by Ethan's reaction that he'd never ride bulls again.

With that swallow, Tanner knew his rodeo career had ended, right there in the Three Rivers arena.

CHAPTER TWO

Summer leaned against the counter at the nurse's station, a chart in front of her but her attention on the conversation between her, Margie, and Belinda.

"She's not saying," Belinda said. A redhead with an eight-month-old baby at home, she only worked two days a week. But they were two of the best days for Summer, who loved Belinda like a sister.

"I'm not sure what that means," Margie said.

Summer's lips curved up even though she told them to stay flat. "It means," she said, keeping her eyes on the numbers on the chart though she'd practically memorized them. "That it's another first date in the books."

"First date, sure." Belinda nudged her with her shoulder. "Is there a second on the horizon?"

Summer abandoned the chart on the countertop. "Surely you forget who you're talking to. The Queen of

First Dates doesn't actually go on *second* dates." She made her voice light and teasing, but her words cut through her core. She hadn't actually been out on a second date in a very long time. She'd stopped counting after her twelfth first date.

"Well, maybe this time will be different." Belinda gave Summer a hopeful look. "I mean, if you want it to be."

"I don't know what I want." Summer picked up the chart and moved to put it back on the door where it belonged. She could be truthful with her friends, and she caught them exchanging a glance when they thought she wasn't looking. "I do know I'm done with cowboys. They have no manners."

Margie stepped into Summer's personal space and gave her a motherly hug. "You'll figure things out."

"How do you know that?" Her whispered question sounded injured, and Summer drew a breath to steady herself. After all, she had meds to deliver and four patients to check on. She didn't have time to feel sorry for herself.

"You're only twenty-six years old," Margie said. "You've got lots of time to figure things out."

"It's not the job, is it?" Belinda asked.

Summer shook her head quickly. "No, I love the job." She cocked her head. "Well, maybe not the swing shift, but now that I have my DVR, even that's not so bad." She sighed. "I'm the youngest in my family and everyone's moved on with their life. I'm the only one still here, still eating Sunday dinner with my parents."

Ethan and Brynn Greene exited from the room beside

her, and she clamped her mouth shut. Brynn had obviously been crying, and while Summer didn't know either of them all that well, she had been going to church with them for the past year and a half.

"How is he?" she asked, her gaze wandering to the closed door of Tanner's room.

"His rodeo career is over." Ethan seemed to look right through her, the anguish on his face genuine and heartbreaking.

"We'll have to wait for the doctor to know for sure." Summer smiled and ducked into the room with the painkillers Tanner needed. He opened his eyes and they took a few seconds to latch onto hers. She'd been a nurse in the Three Rivers Hospital for three years and she could read pain as if it was a book.

"Here you go." She inserted the syringe into the tubes that ran into his hand and pushed the contents into the saline solution entering his body. "You should start to feel better really fast."

His dark eyes seemed fastened on hers, and though she shouldn't, though she had too much work to do in too little time, she paused at his side. Without thinking, she brushed her fingertips along his forehead, pushing back a bit of errant hair. "Let me know if you're not feeling remarkably better within thirty minutes." At least his skin felt normal. Good texture. Proper temperature. "There's a call button right there on the bedrail."

As her hand drifted away from his face, he caught her fingers in his. Slight pressure. Barely there, then gone.

"Thanks," he said, turning his head and letting his eyes fall closed.

She escaped the room, her heart pounding hard against her breastbone. What was she doing? Touching a patient so intimately? She shook her head and inhaled reason into her system. He probably thought nothing of it. Just her checking his temperature or something.

Get me through this shift, she prayed as she set her shoulders and gathered the next chart for the next patient.

AFTER MAKING HER ROUNDS, SHE RETURNED TO the station, where Dr. Verdad stood at the coffee machine. "There you are." He flashed her a brief smile. She wasn't sure if his lips actually curved up or not. She and Belinda had debated his ability to smile at length, and the jury was still out.

He turned from the machine. "I'm ready to see Tanner Wolf."

"Let me grab his chart." She located it on the counter behind her and clicked her pen into action.

"His mother is here," he said. "I met with her briefly in the waiting room before she came back." Dr. Verdad knocked lightly on the door and pushed it open in the next second. "Morning, Tanner." The doctor had excellent bedside manners, and Summer enjoyed working with him. She checked the saline in Tanner's bag and noted his heart rate and temperature while Dr. Verdad shook hands with Tanner's mother.

"Well," he said once the formalities were out of the way. "Has anyone told you what happened?"

"I got gored by a bull," Tanner said, his voice placid.

"Four broken ribs," Dr. Verdad said. "They'll feel better quickly, but you'll have to be careful with them for a long time. They heal slow."

"So I can't ride a horse."

"Not for at least six months." The doctor huffed. "I'm really sorry, Tanner. I know what that means to you."

"How could you possibly know what that means to me?" Tanner's acidic bite matched the flashing anger in his eyes.

Summer's heartbeat blipped unevenly, like the lines on the heart monitor. She watched Dr. Verdad as he studied Tanner and then glanced back at her. She nodded at him, and he sighed. "I was slated to win the Heisman my senior year of college at TCU. Had scouts from all over the NFL coming to watch me play." He stood and lifted his pant leg. "Then I tore my Achilles. I never played football again."

Tanner stared at the scar on Dr. Verdad's leg until the fabric fell over it again. Everything in her felt tight as Dr. Verdad pulled back the thin blanket covering Tanner's body. He wore the standard hospital gown, but the bulk of the tape around his chest and abdomen was obvious, and the cast on his right leg bulged.

"The ribs are a real problem, sure. But you've got your

leg to deal with too. The bull broke the fibula. That's the small bone in the lower leg. I fixed it in surgery with little trouble, and your tibia, miraculously, had only a hairline fracture. I also checked your right ankle, as there are often complications with ankles when the fibula breaks. But all seemed fine. The leg will heal, and it'll heal fast. But I don't think it'll be strong enough to handle bull riding again." He wore the sympathetic smile of someone who understood pain and loss on a personal level. "Maybe horseback riding." He stepped back. "I'm sorry, Tanner."

Summer watched the patient for his reaction. He blinked and breathed, and while his eyes seemed clear of drugs, he certainly wasn't behaving appropriately for one who'd just been told most of his future had been erased. His mother wept, one hand on her son's shoulder.

"So he'll make a full recovery," his mother said through her tears. "He'll be able to walk?"

"With physical therapy, of course." Dr. Verdad nodded to Summer. "He'll only wear that hard cast and use crutches for a week or two, then he'll move into a walking cast. He needs to get out of bed soon, and he can begin his physical therapy as early as tomorrow. Nurse Hamblin here will get him on the schedule."

She nodded, made the notes, and handed the chart to the doctor to sign before he left. He'd get to go back to his office, or maybe to lunch, after this. She'd get over to the physical therapy facilities to schedule Tanner, and then she'd deliver lunch, more medicine, more charts, more more more.

Still, she loved nursing and as she met Tanner's eye before ducking out of his room, she felt something pass between them. A strange understanding or perhaps an acceptance. No matter what it was, it made her blood liquefy and race through her veins.

She went through the motions of her afternoon, her thoughts never straying too far from Tanner. She asked Belinda to get him up and walking that afternoon, too unsure of how she felt. The fact that she felt *anything* was ridiculous. The man didn't actually live in Three Rivers. And she'd never left town except to earn her nursing degree. Even then, she'd promptly scampered back.

Only because of Drew. Just the man's name made her hairline prickle. So she'd had her heart broken. So what? Lots of people did. Lots of people moved on. Yet somehow Summer had moved *back*, started over, gone on first date after first date.

The truth she hadn't told her friends was that she didn't dare go on a second date. Because a second could mean a third, and then she might fall in love with someone only to have him marry her roommate.

CHAPTER THREE

Tanner noticed a marked difference in how he felt the second morning compared to the first. Breathing wasn't easy and according to the doctors and nurses, it wouldn't get better for several months. Broken ribs were no laughing matter, that much was certain. In fact, laughing hurt. Not that Tanner had much opportunity to laugh since waking the previous morning. At least he hadn't sneezed yet.

He hadn't seen the pretty honey-haired nurse again yesterday. A redhead had taken him out walking, and the shift change had landed him with a male nurse with cold hands. Tanner shouldn't care who attended to his health-care needs. He wasn't going to be in the hospital forever. Heck, he wasn't even going to be in Three Rivers very long.

His mother had arrived near the end of the evening, and he'd been glad to see her. He hadn't seen her since starting the rodeo circuit in February. He'd asked about his older brother, but Bill was out of the country for work. And with his wife having just delivered a baby, she'd stayed in Colorado and sent her love with Tanner's mother.

"Morning," a familiar voice chirped, and he glanced away from his phone to find the gorgeous nurse from yesterday.

His phone forgotten, he said, "Morning," and managed a smile.

"You seem better today."

"There's still some pain, especially in my chest."

She nodded, her shoulder-length curls brushing her collarbone. "I'm afraid there will be for a while." She moved around him, checking things and making notes. She didn't touch him again, and he wondered what that first exchange had been about. Summer made easy conversation and he missed her sunshine when she left the room, left him alone.

His mom arrived just after Summer had put breakfast on the rolling tray next to him. His mother kept tucking her hair behind her ear and couldn't seem to sit still in the single recliner next to the bed.

"What's goin' on?" he asked rather than beating around the bush. Never was his style anyway.

"Tanner, I—I have to get back to work soon, and I talked to the doctor, and he said there's no way for you to travel so far so soon."

Tanner frowned, her words tumbling through his head.

"Your friend Ethan said you can stay with him. He has a big house with lots of room. You can keep your place in Colorado Springs, of course. Ethan said he was happy to help you get your horses and everything taken care of. He's coming by this evening, after he gets done out at the ranch."

The more his mother talked, the more confused Tanner became. Finally he said, "Mom, you think I should stay here and recover, is that it?"

Relief ran through her dark eyes. Dark eyes that he saw every time he looked in the mirror. "Yes, dear. Once you're back to normal, you can come back to Colorado Springs and...."

He really wanted her to finish that sentence, because he had no idea what to put into the pregnant pause now lingering between them. He had no idea what to do with his life without the rodeo. The stubborn thought that he could still do the team roping nestled further into his mind. There were more events than bull riding in the rodeo.

Instead of letting a tidal wave of despair engulf him, he reached for his mother's hand and squeezed it. "Okay, Mom. How much longer do you think I have to stay in the hospital?"

"A couple more days." She looked at him with anguish in her face. "I have to get on the road in the morning," she said. "I don't have the kind of job I can just leave."

"You don't need to work, Mom." He'd told her that over and over. Since his father's death six years ago, she'd been working at a grocery store in Colorado Springs. Just enough to pay her bills and live comfortably on the life insurance. Tanner made millions in the rodeo, and his mother wouldn't take a dime of it.

"I can't take care of you anyway," she said. "You'll be better here, with friends and a good home health system."

"Home health?"

"The hospital sends nurses to your house for physical therapy and whatnot."

He wouldn't be doing that, thank you very much. Summer's pretty face traipsed through his mind. Although if *she* was his nurse....

He cleared his throat at the same time he erased the image of her wearing a naughty nurse costume from his traitorous mind. He wasn't that man anymore—at least he didn't want to be. "So Ethan will come by tonight and explain everything."

"He said he would," his mom said.

That sounded exactly like Ethan, who probably had Tanner's horses at his wife's boarding stables, and Tanner's truck and trailer parked in his driveway. He'd have a guest room ready, and a wheelchair ramp built over the front steps before Tanner got released from the hospital. Ethan was nothing if not predictable—and trustworthy, and as close to a saint as Tanner knew.

Whenever he was tempted to return to his old way of life, Tanner thought of Ethan's example. He reminded Tanner that he didn't have to be perfect. Didn't have to have a perfect past, come from a perfect family. But that he needed to keep trying, keep listening, and keep believing.

That afternoon, Summer slipped through the door just as Tanner was about to drift to sleep. "Time for your therapy," she chirped.

"I'm tired," he complained.

"Oh, well, then we don't have to go."

"Really?"

She laughed. "No, not really." She used the automatic control to make the bed sit up higher. "Scootch on over to the edge of the bed."

He hated the weakness in his limbs, hated that he had to put his arm around her shoulder to get on his feet, hated that she of all people had to see the bead of sweat at the effort it took to stand and hear his groan of pain.

She walked him over to his physical therapy, her voice painting melodies in his head. She told him about her family, her older siblings, their family holiday traditions. She told him about eating dinner with her parents every Sunday, and her favorite shift, and why she'd gone into nursing.

Tanner didn't have much to add to the conversation. He liked listening to her talk, and since he'd given up talking about his rodeo achievements, he found he didn't have much to say that held a woman's interest anyway.

"All right," she said when they arrived. "Jean will be back to get you in an hour." She signed something on the counter and passed it to the woman standing there.

"Wait," he said as she turned to leave. "Jean's coming

to get me?" He wasn't sure who Jean was, only that she wasn't Summer.

Summer smiled, those teeth and lips once again distracting him. "Yes, my shift is over right now." She yawned like she'd been there since dawn. Maybe she had been. The hours seemed to warp together to Tanner.

"Oh, all right." Tanner tried to mask the disappointment in his voice, but he failed. Summer held his gaze for a breath past comfortable, then she lifted her hand in an awkward wave and left.

Tanner berated himself for his stupidity. So he'd spent a few minutes with a pretty nurse. Didn't mean anything. Still, the only way he made it through the next hour of torture and pain was by focusing on the shape of her face, remembering the clean, fresh scent of her hair, listening to the sound of her voice in his head.

By the time Ethan showed up, Tanner was tired, hungry, and very cranky. He listened to his friend outline the plan, and he didn't put up a fight about it. His trailer and truck were at Ethan's. His horses were out at Three Rivers Ranch. Ethan had taken care of everything, just as Tanner had suspected he would.

And he owed it to Ethan to show his gratitude. "Thanks," he said, his voice tight in his throat. "You didn't have to do all this."

"I know I didn't." Ethan watched him with anxiety galloping through his green eyes. "So what are you going to do now?"

Tanner took a deep breath. "I guess my rodeo days are

over." The back of his throat felt like it was coated with sawdust, and he couldn't believe his last rodeo had taken place in tiny Three Rivers, the speck of a town in the Texas panhandle he'd only visited twice before.

"You won the team roping event." Ethan studied the whiteboard where Tanner's medications and schedule had been written. "And you could rope again. Not this year. But again."

"I've still never ridden Lucky Number Thirteen." Tanner couldn't decide how his voice sounded. He didn't feel particularly angry, or devastated, or heartbroken. He just felt and sounded…hollow.

"Don't hate me." Ethan stood and put his cowboy hat back on like he was getting ready to leave. "But maybe you weren't meant to ride him. Maybe being here in Three Rivers is what's really lucky."

Tanner riddled through his words. "Because I have you and Brynn to take care of me?"

"That's one reason, sure." Ethan ducked his head and said, "I'll be back tomorrow night. I'll see your ma off in the mornin' too." He reached for the door and had it open before Tanner could get his mouth to work.

"Ethan," he called.

His friend turned back, his face open and unassuming.

"Thank you." Tanner gave him a weak smile, which Ethan returned before leaving so the door could fall closed behind him. Tanner hated the silence that came with Ethan's departure. And not even true silence, but a noth- ingness punctuated with the humming of machines and the occasional beeping from his monitors. At least he didn't have the IV anymore, or the throat tube, or anything else restricting him to bed.

He got up, intending to get as strong as possible before he left the hospital. *I won't be a burden to Brynn and Ethan for long,* he vowed as he entered the hall and began walking the circuit around the floor.

CHAPTER FOUR

Summer enjoyed her day off by spending time in her garden and yard. Pruning bushes and eliminating weeds always brought a sense of satisfaction she couldn't get anywhere else. Maybe as she bandaged wounds and administered pain relievers, as she watched patients get back on their feet and restart their lives.

She thought about Tanner Wolf, wondering why he of all people had wormed his way into her mind when she helped dozens of patients each week. Something about his dark eyes called to her. Something in them spoke of good times tinged with bad, of excitement dulled by tragedy, of power edged with temperance.

When she went into work the following day, she found Tanner's chart in the discharge pile. She picked it up and leafed through it. He'd been walking more than his physical therapy required, and she noticed that he'd been enrolled in the home health program. With four broken ribs that would take months to heal, not to mention the broken leg, his name on the home health list wasn't surprising.

She noted that a nurse hadn't been assigned to him yet, and his discharge papers still needed to be signed by Dr. Verdad. Her heart jumped in a peculiar way, tripling when Belinda came around the corner, her car keys jangling.

"Good morning," she sang as she shoved her purse into the closet behind the nurse's station.

Summer dropped Tanner's chart like it had been coated in acid, the metal on the clipboard clattering on the counter. Belinda looked at it and back to Summer. She grabbed it before Summer could cover it and danced away with a giggle.

"Belinda," Summer warned.

She scanned the chart. "Ah, Tanner Wolf." She met Summer's eyes. "Daydreaming about date number two with the handsome cowboy?"

Summer folded her arms and cocked her hip. "There'd have to be a date number one for that to happen."

"Oh, there has been." Belinda put the file back and checked her assignment for the day. "He's on my rotation. Want to switch?"

Summer wanted to blurt, "Yes!" but she sucked the word back into her throat. Belinda picked up the white-board eraser and removed Tanner's name from her list. She used the red marker to add it to Summer's, stopping short of drawing a heart next to his name.

"You should go see him," she said. "Date number two."

Summer rolled her eyes. "What was date number one?"

"You taking him over to his physical therapy appointment."

"That wasn't a date." Summer reached for the coffee pot to busy herself so she didn't have to meet her friend's all-knowing gaze. "And how did you know that? You weren't even here."

"I have my ways." Belinda giggled. "And you've never taken patients to their physical therapy."

"Yes, I have." Summer's hand trembled the tiniest bit as she added sugar to her coffee.

"Name one time."

Summer pressed her lips together, her mind cycling through the countless patients she'd worked with in the three years she'd been in the recovery ward. "Gwendolyn."

"She doesn't count."

"Why not?"

"She's your brother's wife."

"I still walked her over to the physical therapy unit."

"And no one else until Mister Tanner Wolf."

"He seemed like he could use a friend. That's all." Summer sipped her coffee and found it too bitter, despite the copious spoonfuls of sugar she'd added. She set it aside, her stomach rioting against the liquid anyway.

Belinda bumped her with her hip. "It's okay to like him."

"I don't like him," Summer said, though she actually did. "He's a patient, that's all."

"Ah, good morning, ladies." Dr. Brady stepped over to the coffee pot. "Staff meeting in five minutes. Everyone else is in there."

Summer followed Belinda into the staff room, where Dr. Brady had his weekend pastries already set out. Summer took a seat beside Margie and crossed her arms, like that would keep the brewing storm in her chest contained.

Dr. Brady talked about the assignments and the discharges. Summer only had Tanner on her list of patients being released that day, and she said she'd contact Dr. Verdad to get the paperwork going.

"It looks like he'll be receiving home health," Dr. Brady said next. "Who's available for that?" He glanced at his notes. "He'll need someone every day for the first two weeks, then three times a week for six more. Then we'll re-evaluate."

Belinda kicked Summer under the table, and she emitted a yelp of surprise. Dr. Brady focused on her. "Summer? You want to take Tanner's case?"

Summer forgot how to speak. She only breathed because it was involuntary and she didn't have to think about doing it.

"Yes," Belinda said. "Yes, she does."

Dr. Brady scratched something on his paper. "Summer Hamblin for Tanner Wolf. All right, let's see. We have Mister Thompson coming in this afternoon. He'll need a patient nurse." He glanced up. "Margie?"

Summer laughed with everyone else as Margie steadfastly shook her head no. Dale Thompson seemed to be a regular in their wing, and he was cranky and combative on a good day. So the day he had surgery tended to show a side of him few could weather.

"I'll help her," Summer said, though the last time she'd worked with Dale, he'd thrown a full cup of water at her and ordered her to never come back.

"You're just full of surprises today," Dr. Brady said as he made another note.

Summer startled and turned to Belinda. "What does that mean?"

"Probably that you never volunteer for difficult assignments, nor have you been out for homecare in over a year." She smirked at Summer.

"Maybe I'm turning over a new leaf." Summer sniffed and shifted away from Belinda.

"Maybe you'll be dating before you know it." She stood with the other nurses, somehow keeping up with the meeting and the conversation. Summer watched her go, wondering how Belinda knew everything Summer thought or felt. Maybe she wore her emotions on her face, too easy for everyone to read.

She collected Tanner's chart, along with her wits, and knocked on his door. "Good morning," she said as she entered and found him sitting up in bed. He clicked off the TV and grinned at her. The power of his smile at full wattage nearly knocked her backward. She stumbled at the sight of his tan face, his short stubble, his straight teeth. Without pain to hamper him, without drugs to subdue him, he was glorious and handsome.

"Morning. I didn't see you yesterday."

"It was my day off." She took his temperature and pulse, making notes on his chart. "You're set to be released today. Doctor Verdad just needs to come over and meet with you."

"I'm not in a hurry," he said. "I have friends coming to pick me up, but they can't come until this afternoon."

"All right." Summer wrote on his chart. "I'll tell Doctor Verdad that. I also see that you'll be receiving home health for eight weeks to help with the recovery. Where will you be staying?"

"With Ethan Greene. Do you know where he lives?"

"Built a house on the west edge of town, I think. What's the address?"

Tanner chuckled, but nervousness filled the sound. "I don't really know. I was supposed to go see the house after the rodeo, and well...."

"I'll ask him," she said to fill the uncomfortable silence. "How long will you be staying with him?"

"I don't know." Tanner leaned his head back against his pillow. "Hopefully not very long."

Summer looked at him, directly at him, something she hadn't allowed herself to do yet. "So will you not be using the full eight weeks of home health?"

"I sure hope not," he said darkly.

"Because you'll be leaving town? I mean, you don't live here, right?"

His eyes flashed, but Sumer couldn't quite read the emotion in them. "I have a place in Colorado Springs," he said. "But I'm hardly there anyway. I suppose it won't matter if I stay here for eight weeks, or ten, or forever."

Must be nice, she thought. She couldn't imagine having houses all over the country, or not having to worry about paying for them. She cleared her jealous thoughts and said, "So is that a yes to the eight weeks of home health? It's usually best to commit to the full term."

"I think I can manage myself," he said. "Ethan and Brynn will be there to help me."

Disappointment cut through Summer. "All right," she said airily. "I'll tell the doctor to assign me to someone else." She turned to leave his bedside, but his fingers curled around her forearm.

Heat rushed through her body like she'd been dipped in pure sunshine. She sucked in a breath that echoed through the quiet room and focused on the point of contact. His large hand gripped her arm with a gentleness she didn't know a man so bulky could possess.

She looked back at Tanner and found a flush in his face. He blinked and the spell between them broke. "You're going to be my home health nurse?" His fingers slipped from her skin, leaving her cold and empty.

"I was assigned this morning, yes."

"Assigned," he repeated, his voice softening.

Summer didn't know how to tell him she'd desperately

wanted his case but had been too afraid to volunteer herself. So she simply said, "Your breakfast should be up in a few minutes," and got out of there before she did something completely inappropriate—like kiss him.

She pressed her back against his closed door and *breathed.* Breathed like she'd forgotten how when she'd entered his presence. Margie exited the room next door, startling Summer into her next task. Maybe being Tanner's homecare nurse was a bad idea. She tried to convince herself to find Dr. Brady and ask him to assign someone else as she made her rounds, gave out meds, and started delivering breakfast.

She entered Tanner's room and found him sitting in the recliner instead of the bed. "Look at you." She grinned and set his breakfast on the rolling tray.

"I'll commit to the eight weeks of homecare," he said, his eyes boring straight into hers. "If you promise not to treat me like I'm about to break."

She pushed the cart in front of him and leaned into it. "Mister Wolf, by the time I'm finished with you, you'll wish you'd never said those words." She grinned and started laughing, glad when his deep chuckle mingled with hers.

"After I finish eating, will you walk with me?" he asked.

She pretended to check something on the monitor behind him though he wasn't hooked up to it. "Sure," she said. "But you have physical therapy at ten this morning."

"And you'll walk me over there?"

"Sure."

"Good, because yesterday some guy came and got me, and I didn't like it nearly as much as you tellin' me about your life." He grinned at her, something dangerous and electric in his eyes just before he dropped them to his plate of food. "Oh, and I'm gonna need more to eat than this. I swear you're trying to starve me here."

"Well, most of our patients aren't as…big as you."

"Are you saying I'm fat?" He grinned, that twinkle in his eye downright charming. It stole her breath and made her abandon her status as Queen of First Dates. She wanted a lot of dates with this man.

She giggled and put a couple of steps between them so she wasn't inhaling the manly scent of his skin. All those manly pheromones clouded her reason. "You just have more muscles than we normally see on our patients."

"Well, wrestling a four-hundred-pound calf to the ground ain't easy." He frowned and his countenance darkened. "Of course, walking ain't easy right now."

Compassion filled her, almost choking her. "You'll get back to where you were," she said.

He shook his head. "Nope. Not gonna ride again."

"Maybe not in a rodeo," Summer said, her heart expanding for this man. "But surely you'll be able to ride a horse again. You could rope."

Tanner met her eye and held it. "We'll see."

"Yes, we will." She gave him a careful smile, one she hoped didn't come across as too flirty. "I'll see you later, okay? Ring me if you need anything."

CHAPTER FIVE

Tanner wanted to ring for Summer every other minute. He constantly talked himself out of pushing that blasted button. He didn't need pain medication, and he could get up and get his own drink of water.

After a half an hour of arguing with himself he got up and left his room. She'd said she'd walk with him, but he didn't see her at the nurse's station. He didn't want to ask after her, thinking that too obvious when he'd been traipsing around the floor alone for a couple of days without her. So he set his feet to walking as best as he could, trying to employ the strategies he'd learned in his physical therapy over the past two sessions.

He tired quickly but decided to go around one more time, his hopes hovering near the clouds that he'd see Summer. She came out of his room as he rounded the corner, her expression worried.

"Hey," he called, immediately cursing himself for practically yelling at her from down the hall.

Relief eased her features back to their usual gorgeousness. "There you are." She strode toward him. "You have physical therapy in an hour. You shouldn't be up."

"I said I wanted to go for a walk. You were supposed to come with me." He put his hand on her arm and leaned on her. "I should've brought a stand or something."

She moved closer to him and lent him her strength. "You shouldn't have gone so far."

"I'll be okay." He wanted to lift his arm over her shoulders, but the thought of what pain would cascade through his ribs was enough to keep him from doing so.

And he was okay through physical therapy. He'd asked Summer about the church in town, and she spent the walk to the PT unit talking about the pastor, the people, the picnics. He wanted to experience them all, and when she came to pick him up, he asked, "Can I go to church with you next week?"

She stalled, her step pausing before picking up again. "Well, Ethan and Brynn go every week."

"Oh, sure they do." Tanner focused on the end of the hallway, every cell in his body tired. He probably had overdone it with the walking this morning, doubled with the physical therapy. Suddenly the possibility of the male aide pushing him back to his room in a wheelchair sounded great.

He wasn't sure how to say he didn't want to go to church with Ethan and Brynn. In a lot of ways, he felt far inferior to Ethan, like he'd never measure up. He'd dismissed the fleeting thoughts as they tried to infiltrate his mind over the past months. He did again now, replacing those negative feelings with a sense of gratitude instead.

Still, he wanted to sit by Summer at church. He liked her smile, enjoyed the way she put him at ease, wanted to breathe in the floral undertone of her scent. "Can I sit by you anyway?" he asked, deciding to be brave and lay a couple of cards on the table. "Or do you have someone you sit by? You know, a boyfriend or someone?" He resolutely kept his eyes on the elevator bank at the end of the hall.

Summer tipped her head back and laughed, the sound delicious and carefree in Tanner's ears. "I don't have a boyfriend."

"Oh, well, then the seat next to you is open, right?"

"I usually sit by my parents."

"You have two sides." Tanner realized he was being relentless, and part of him angered. Why was it so hard to overcome the man he'd been? If she didn't want to sit by him, she didn't have to sit by him.

They reached the elevator and Summer pushed the button to call the car. "I do have two sides, Mister Wolf, and I'd love to sit by you at church." She beamed up at him, the sincerity in her blue eyes diving straight into his heart.

Tanner got discharged that afternoon, and the drive to Ethan's house nearly undid his composure. He'd slept for hours, but his ribs did *not* like the tiny jostles of the truck. Even the slightest bump sent pain from front to back. He was panting by the time Ethan pulled alongside his truck.

The house before them fit Ethan to a T. Dark gray siding and white trim, with a black garage door, the house rose two stories above ground with a beautiful lawn.

"Thanks for bringing my stuff here," Tanner said, spying his horse trailer on the side of the garage.

"Brynn has dinner ready," Ethan said, but he made no move to get out of the truck. "I wanted to ask you if you wanted to go out to Courage Reins. Not right away, but maybe once your ribs can handle it."

"Courage Reins? That's the therapeutic center, right?"

"Right." Ethan twisted and looked at him.

"I'm fine, Ethan." Tanner reached for the door handle, unwilling to have this conversation today. No, he hadn't come to terms with everything he'd lost, but he didn't need to right away.

Ethan waited for him at the front of the truck, which annoyed Tanner. He could walk into the house by himself. Ethan didn't touch him, didn't try to coach him up the front steps, just followed him, his steady breathing almost as much of a comfort as it was an annoyance.

"The guest room is in the basement," Ethan said. "If that doesn't work, you can take our bedroom."

"I'm not taking your bedroom," Tanner growled. "The basement's fine."

Brynn wiped her hands on her apron as she came out of the kitchen. "Tanner." Her smile was made of nerves as she stretched up to kiss his cheek. "I made hamburgers and potato salad."

"You can cook?" he asked in a playful tone.

"Hey." She swatted at his bicep and he started to flinch away when a sharp pain radiated through his core. He groaned and her face paled. "Come sit down."

"I'm fine," he said, though his breath came quick and left quicker. He hobbled to the kitchen table and sat in a chair, the cast on his lower leg a heavy burden. He reminded himself that he'd only have to wear it for a week or so, determined to find all the silver linings he could.

Ethan joined Brynn in the kitchen and he sliced tomatoes while she murmured to him about making over-easy eggs for the hamburgers. Tanner knew the egg was for him—he loved a fried egg on his hamburger, and both Brynn and Ethan knew it.

He didn't tell them they didn't need to make the eggs. Everything seemed too heavy for him at the moment. Living with them. Trying to get around by himself. Being responsible for his own pain care. Everything.

He managed to make it through dinner and get down to the guest room. Ethan had set up a TV across from the bed, and the bathroom was right across the hall. Tanner wouldn't have to go upstairs unless he wanted to get to the kitchen, and Brynn said she'd bring his food down to him. Whatever was easiest.

They left, and Tanner made himself as comfortable as possible in the bed. What would be easiest would to be whole again. His thoughts spiraled into fury, and he stared at the dark TV. "Why did this happen to me?" he whispered, finally allowing the reality of his future to fully cover him.

No more rodeo.

No more roping.

No more bull riding.

No more traveling.

Tanner had been on the rodeo circuit for twelve years—his entire adult life. He had no idea how to live in one place for more than a couple of months. No idea how to do much besides train a horse and throw a rope. He had no college education, no technical experience.

Doesn't matter, he told himself. He'd been reckless in his past, wild even. But not with his money. He had plenty to live on, probably for the rest of his life.

"Still can't lie around all day," he muttered to himself. His emotions seemed to be on a roller coaster, first soaring toward fury, then settling toward acceptance, all within the timespan of a heartbeat.

True, he didn't need a job to survive. He was lucky that way. But he did need something to do with his life. Some sort of purpose.

As he closed his eyes and wished for sleep, he prayed

that God would let him know what he should do with his life now that he didn't have the rodeo.

The next morning, he got up early so he could be ready for church on time. He waited on the couch in a pair of Ethan's slacks and one of Ethan's black-and-white plaid shirts. The clothes fit well enough, if Tanner wasn't all that worried about the fabric pulling across his shoulders and the pants not quite reaching the floor the way they should. He had about forty pounds on Ethan, a couple of inches, and broader shoulders.

"You're ready already?" Ethan asked as he came padding out of his bedroom. "We don't have to leave for an hour."

"Didn't want anyone waitin' on me. I even made coffee." He lifted the mug he'd poured for himself. He wouldn't tell Ethan he was already so tired that he wanted to go back to bed for a few hours. He also hadn't told Ethan about his arrangement to sit with the pretty, available Summer Hamblin.

No time like the present, he thought.

Ethan finished pouring his coffee and joined Tanner in the living room. "So, once we get to church, I need to find Summer Hamblin," Tanner said.

Ethan choked and slopped his coffee onto the back of his hand, bolted to standing, and hurried into the kitchen. He ran cold water over his hand and cleaned up his coffee spill. "Summer Hamblin?"

"She said I could sit by her."

Ethan got over his initial shock and started laughing. "Leave it to you to find a date in the hospital."

"It's not a date," Tanner said. "It's church. You're the one who said I should go."

"Absolutely you should. How long you been goin'?"

"About a year."

Ethan beamed at him. "Good for you, Tanner. How's it going?"

Tanner exhaled and took another sip of his coffee. "Slower than I thought, actually. You make everything look easy." He slid Ethan a mock glare.

His friend chuckled. "Change is always easier on the outside," he said. "It took me a while too. You'll get there." He refilled his coffee cup and came back into the living room. "And Summer Hamblin is a nice girl."

"You know her?"

"Superficially. See her at church every week. Her brothers are big rodeo fans." Ethan threw him a grin. "So you have that going for you."

"Not in the rodeo anymore, remember?" Tanner wished his words didn't have quite so much bite.

"It's not all lost yet." Someone knocked on the door as Ethan finished speaking. He glanced toward it with puzzlement on his face.

"Wonder who that could be." Ethan got up to answer the door, blocking who stood on the porch. A higher, feminine voice reached Tanner's ears, but never in a million years did he expect Ethan to step back to allow Daisy Keller entrance to his house.

Tanner couldn't even get up and hide. So he sat rooted in place, everything inside him icing over. "What are you doing here?" he asked as she drew nearer. He hadn't seen Daisy in probably two years. She'd been his last fling before he'd decided to give religion a try. Their relationship hadn't ended well, to say the least.

"I heard about your accident," she said. Her voice didn't belong in Texas. Didn't have enough twang, enough sway to the words. "I came to see how you were doing. Your mama said you were staying here."

"I'm fine." Tanner switched his gaze to Ethan, silently pleading for him to get Daisy out of here.

"Ethan," Brynn called. "Are you showering or can I get in?"

"Coming," Ethan said. "I'll let you two get caught up." He continued past Tanner, clearly misinterpreting the glare Tanner sent him.

"You should go," Tanner said as soon as Ethan's bedroom door closed.

Daisy laughed. "I'm not going to go. It took me two days to get here." She glanced around Ethan's house like it held more manure than she liked. "This place is out in the middle of nowhere."

"I like it," Tanner said automatically. Anything not to agree with her. "We'll be leaving for church in a few minutes. I don't have time to talk right now."

"I'll go to church with you." She smiled at him all sugar sweet, and Tanner wondered what she wanted. They'd dated for six months before he'd realized he wanted more out of his life, before he'd realized how happy Ethan and Brynn were, before he'd realized that he wanted what they had.

Daisy had not been religious when they'd been together. Looking at her now, Tanner knew she still wasn't. "What do you want?" he asked.

"Nothing." Her pink-painted nails slid up his arm. "Just wanted to see how you were doing."

"I'm fine."

"When will you go back to Colorado Springs?"

Deciding right then and there, Tanner said, "I'm not. I'm going to stay here. Ethan's helping me for a few weeks until I can find my own place."

"So you'll sell your place in Colorado Springs?"

Understanding flooded Tanner's mind. "That's why you came. You want my house in Colorado."

She pulled her hand back and looked away. "I care about you, Tanner."

He laughed, which sent an ache through his chest. "Sure you do."

Brynn came out of the bedroom dressed and ready for church. "Let me grab some coffee and we'll go." She glanced at Daisy as if she didn't know the woman was there. "Oh, hello. I'm Brynn. I don't think we've met."

"Daisy." She nodded at Brynn. "I'm Tanner's...." She glanced at him. "Friend," she finished.

Brynn searched Tanner's face for confirmation, but he gave her none. "Ethan will be out in a minute. You want to start getting in the truck, Tanner?"

"I can take him," Daisy said.

"No," Tanner said. "It's fine."

"I insist."

Panic pounded through Tanner. He didn't truly believe Daisy would dare go into church with him. He didn't have Summer's number to text her. So he arrived at church with Daisy hanging on him like she was the one who couldn't walk, and he couldn't even warn Summer.

She happened to be twisted around, looking at the door when he went through it. He seemed drawn to her by some inexplicable force, and they locked eyes. Summer's traveled down his shoulder to his arm, where Daisy clung to him. Shock colored her face, and she whipped around to face the front before Tanner could shrug Daisy's grip off his arm.

Tanner suffered through the sermon, getting nothing from it that he hoped he would. He'd hoped God would answer his prayers about what to do with his life now that he didn't have the rodeo. He'd hoped to feel the peace and comfort he often had at church. He'd hoped to maybe even be brave enough to hold Summer's hand.

The service ended, and Tanner stood as quickly as his injuries would allow. "Stay here," he commanded. "I need to go talk to a friend."

"You have friends here?" Daisy asked as he limped away, the crutches an annoyance he wanted to toss away. He ignored Daisy, his mission to get to Summer before she could escape singular. He reached the end of her row before she left, boxing her in.

"Hey," he said. He didn't know Summer that well, but he somehow knew he better talk fast. "I'm so sorry. This old friend of mine showed up out of nowhere today. She's leaving right after lunch. You're coming tonight, right?"

"Five o'clock," Summer said clinically. "Of course, if that doesn't work…or if your friend can help you, that's totally fine."

He hated that she wouldn't look at him, that so many people loitered around them, talking and cleaning up after their kids.

"Summer." He reached for her hand and took her fingers in his. He rejoiced to be touching her, though the touch was simple and much more chaste than what he normally did. "I'm sorry. I didn't know she was coming."

She lifted her eyes to his. "You asked me if I had a boyfriend," she said. "I guess it never occurred to me that you'd have a girlfriend."

"I don't," he insisted. "She's not—" He glanced back to where Daisy sat staring a hole through Summer. "I've been thinking about a specific woman a lot lately, but it isn't her."

"Summer," a woman said from behind Tanner. He glanced at the redheaded nurse who'd made him get out of bed that first day in the hospital. She balanced a baby on her hip. "You coming to the picnic?"

Tanner dropped Summer's hand. "Summer, please," he whispered.

"Five o'clock," she repeated, a beautiful flush rising through her face. "Excuse me." She slipped past him and into the aisle as she cooed at the baby the redhead held. She took the boy and they moved down the aisle. Tanner watched them go, hope and gladness shooting through him when Summer turned back to him when she reached the doorway. She smiled halfway, and Tanner lifted his hand in an acknowledgement wave.

Now he just had to get rid of Daisy. Fast.

CHAPTER SIX

*D*ate number four. Belinda's teasing voice wouldn't leave Summer's ears. She didn't know what she was doing. Holding the man's hand in church. Being so hopeful to sit by him during a sermon. Allowing herself to be so devastated when he'd walked in with another woman. She barely knew the man's middle name. She had no right to feel so attached to him, so possessive of him.

And yet, she did. She sat in her car in Ethan Greene's driveway, the air conditioning keeping the Texas heat out, as she waited for the final minutes to tick toward five o'clock.

One hour, she told herself.

Sixty minutes.

Thirty-six hundred seconds.

She would only stay for one hour. That was what she got paid for, and she would do her job and go home. Or rather, to her parents' for dinner. Her oldest brother was in town for the weekend, so at least she wouldn't be alone. No, she'd have two nieces to talk with while the adults enjoyed their conversation.

With five minutes left, Tanner appeared on the front porch, only using one crutch on his right side. The weight of his gaze reached across the lawn and through the windshield. Giving up on waiting, she got out of her car, sweaty before she'd taken three steps.

"You've been out here for ten minutes," he said.

"Wasn't sure if you'd be ready until five." She climbed the steps under his scrutiny.

"I'm ready," he said, and she was sure he wasn't talking about his physical therapy.

"You've been walking?"

"As instructed."

"So, typically our first visit is an assessment of the living conditions so we can gauge future needs."

"Ethan has me in his guest room in the basement."

Summer frowned, a spike of concern poking through her. "The basement? Tanner, that's not good."

"I can manage the stairs."

She shook her head. "No, they're too much for you right now." She slid her assessing gaze down his body and back to his eyes. "You shouldn't be putting so much weight on your leg yet."

"I'm fine. And I'm not kicking them out of their room."

"Then you need to get your own place." Her eyes

danced toward his and away again before she could get sucked into the dark depths of them. "You have the means to get your own apartment? Maybe a single-level house?"

When he didn't answer right away, she looked at him. She gravitated a bit closer to him. "Do you?"

"Yes," he said. "Did you know you're really pretty?"

Every cell in her body ignited. "Thank you, Tanner." She cleared her throat, feeling anything but pretty next to him. His good looks shrouded anyone else nearby in shadow. "I can help you find a place. We can look this afternoon if you have time."

"Summer, I have nothing but time."

"Great." She hurried down the steps away from him. Being so close was proving to be so dangerous. From the woodsy scent of his cologne to that sexy cowboy hat, and all she could think about was touching him again, kissing him, going out with him over and over again.

She remembered her training when she reached the sidewalk. Turning, she said, "Do you need help?"

"Not yours," he said as he took the steps one at a time to join her. He laced his fingers through hers and squeezed. "Is this okay?"

"Uh huh," she said dumbly before remembering that she was not some silly schoolgirl. "I mean, sure."

"There's no policy about nurses dating their patients?"

Her feet froze to the sidewalk though the temperature had to be hovering near triple digits. "Dating?"

"Yeah, I'm…interested." He lifted their joined hands a

few inches and let them fall with an awkward chuckle. "Obviously."

"But I don't date." She didn't understand the anxiety accelerating through her. Only knew it was there, and it was screaming at her to run in the opposite direction.

"At all?"

She shook her head. "It's a long story."

"Like I said, I have nothing but time." He gave her a kind smile, and she wondered if maybe the cowboys she'd been out with lately had simply been cut from different cloth than Tanner.

"All right," she said. "I actually do go out quite a bit. But usually only once, and well, I haven't had a second date in months."

"That's just fine with me," he teased. "Is this a date?"

"No." She laughed. "I'm getting paid right now."

"So, after six o'clock, then. Can we go to dinner then? Would that be a date?"

She ducked her head, wanting to tuck herself into this man's strong side. "Yeah, I think that would be a date."

She waited for him to settle into the passenger seat of her car and then she closed the door behind him so he wouldn't have to reach and stretch his injured ribs. When she joined him in the car, he held his phone toward her. "If you put your number in that, I promise to call tomorrow."

Equal parts giddiness and fear paraded through her. She was interested too, though, so she typed in the digits and handed the phone back. Hers chimed as she backed out of the driveway.

"That's me," he said. "Now you have my number too."

She pulled to the side of the road and collected her phone, the nearness of him, the way he filled the car physically and otherwise, made her head swim. She cleared it and said, "Okay, so I wasn't prepared to go house shopping tonight. Let's look at what's available right now." She pulled up a real estate app and put in the zip code for Three Rivers. "Thirteen properties," she murmured.

"Lucky number thirteen," he said, his voice so quiet she barely heard it.

"Is that your lucky number?" she asked, watching him.

He didn't smile, and his eyes didn't hold their usual light. "No, that was the name of the bull who changed my life."

Summer pressed her lips together. "I'm sorry, Tanner."

"I like how you say my name."

"How do I say your name?" She glanced at him.

"Like you care about me." He drank her in, and she couldn't look away from him though every reasonable fiber of her being shouted at her to do so.

"I do care about you," she said, her voice a ghost of itself.

"You're a nurse," he said, his head dipping a bit closer to hers. "You care about everyone."

"That's a myth," she said even as he inched closer. "I'm a person too. I like and dislike people just like you do. I just don't show it at work."

His fingers combed through her hair and rested on her collarbone briefly. "Are you working right now?"

"No." She felt mesmerized by him, completely taken by his charm, his good looks, his tragic accident.

"Can I kiss you then?"

"I don't normally kiss on the first date." She would not tell him that Belinda had labeled this as date number four. She would not.

"You said this wasn't a date."

"I *definitely* don't kiss *before* the first date." She smiled and ducked her head, causing Tanner to drop his hand. She wanted to kiss him, and yet the prospect also terrified her. She hadn't kissed a man in longer than she'd been on a second date with one. She wouldn't be telling him that either.

Summer pushed the fire climbing through her core back where it belonged. "So, thirteen options. This one's on the second floor. That's out. This one needs heavy remodeling...." Fifteen minutes later, she'd shown him five places on the app, and they'd decided to go drive by as many as they could before dinner.

As they walked up to the front door of the third house, Summer's stomach growled. Tanner glanced at her. "Want to go eat after this?"

"You know what?" She faced him. "I forgot that I'm eating at my parents' tonight. My brother is in town with his family, and I said I'd be there."

His face fell, his hopes practically shattering on the ground at her feet. "Okay, another time then."

"Maybe you'd like to come to dinner at my parents' house," she said. "I think we have time to poke around here. My mother said six-thirty."

A bright smile nearly rendered her weak. "Sure, I'd like that." As quick as he'd brightened, he dimmed. "I mean, if your father isn't the kind of Texan man who answers the door with a loaded gun." He peered at her. "Is he?"

She tipped her head back and laughed, the second time Tanner had been able to elicit such a response from her. She loved that he could make her laugh, loved how free she felt when she did. "My parents have been nagging me to get married for a couple of years now. I think he'll welcome you with open arms and try to get you to propose before dessert." She turned toward the house, but then fell back a step. "Oh, and my brother just might be your biggest fan."

His face paled, and she giggled. "Bet you're regretting accepting the invitation so quickly now, aren't you?" She watched him without making it obvious, hoping for a reaction that said he didn't care about her father, or her brother, or her mother. Just her.

"Will it still count as a date?" he asked.

"Sure," she said. "Isn't taking someone home to meet your parents the ultimate date?"

"So maybe it'll count as three or four dates," he said, that dangerous glint she'd seen before entering his eyes.

"Why does it matter?"

"How many dates do you usually go on before kissing someone?"

"Well, I—" She clamped her mouth closed around the confession that her lips had been virgin for quite some time. She leaned toward him, her desire to kiss him close to spilling over, close to allowing her to abandon all reason, close to kissing him right here, right now, on someone else's doorstep.

"About five," she said breathlessly. She settled back onto her own feet and faced the door. She smoothed down her shirt and took a deep breath to center herself. "Now, let's see if this house is the one for you."

By the time they arrived at Summer's parent's house, her nerves felt like they'd been doused in gasoline and lit on fire. What had she been thinking? She hadn't brought a man home for dinner in well, years.

Her mother would go into combat mode, and her father would ask too many questions, and her sister-in-law—true fear gripped her stomach. Gwendolyn was the queen of innuendo, and Summer sat in the driveway with her fingers clenched around the wheel.

"Are we going to go in?" Tanner faced the front of the red-brick house without a trace of fear. He swung his gaze to her, and she swallowed.

"Might as well, I guess."

"We don't have to," he said. "I saw a diner back there that was open."

"Nice try." She tossed him a wry smile. "I just…."

He took her hand in his and all her fears fled. "Haven't dated in a while. I heard the first time. It's no big deal."

"I only know your middle name because I saw it on your chart."

He blinked and then started to laugh, cutting the sound off with a groan. He pressed his elbows to his ribs. "Don't make me laugh. It hurts."

She stared sourly out the windshield again, unsure why her nerves were boiling now. Over this. "My middle name is Renee, in case you wanted to know."

"I did." He reached for the door handle. "I want to know everything about you."

Her fear warmed, but she still prayed for patience to make it through the evening with her family. As predicted, her mother gushed over Tanner's presence at the dinner table. Her brother peppered him with questions about the rodeo circuit and the other cowboys while her sister-in-law kept whispering comments about his handsomeness to Summer.

Her father beamed at the lot of them, visions of summer weddings in his eyes. It was all too much for Summer after about thirty minutes, but she kept her smile hitched in place. She told her family she was helping Tanner find somewhere more suitable to live; he said he was looking to make a fresh start in Three Rivers; Gwendolyn and Rob announced they were having another baby just before Christmas.

By the time she spilled into the summer night, the

moon was arcing through the sky and it was dark enough for it to light the whole sky.

Tanner sighed as he positioned himself on her right and once again took her hand in his. "That was really great."

"You don't have to lie."

"I'm not." He cut her a glance out of the corner of his eye. "Better than lying in bed, watching reruns for hours on end."

"You're not too tired?"

"I'm utterly exhausted." He yawned as he leaned on the crutch and stepped. "But I have nothing on my schedule tomorrow, so I think I'll have time to recover."

She unlocked the car so he could get in. "You have physical therapy exercises," she reminded him. "And I'm working until three-thirty, so I'll be by after that."

"I'll get the physical therapy done, nurse." He flashed her a teasing smile.

"Just doing my job." She got in and started the car. When they got back to Ethan's, she wasn't sure if she should help him up the front steps or just drop him off. The protocol was blurred, as she wasn't on-duty, but if she was, she'd help him in, assess the bedroom, all of it.

She chose to get out of the car. "I still haven't seen your living conditions." She grabbed his file from the backseat. "I have to report on them."

"Come on in, then." His smile this time held more than friendship, more than teasing, and her pulse pounded in a way it hadn't in years.

CHAPTER SEVEN

Tanner wasn't sure how he could make it through five dates with the fun, flirty, fantastic Summer Hamblin before kissing her. Still, part of him didn't want to go too fast either. He wanted to know if he could be attracted to a woman physically and take the time to get to know her. He hated to admit that it was a new concept for him—and why he hadn't really tried to have a relationship in the past year.

Summer observed the room Ethan had provided for him, her mouth turned down and her eyes firing up.

"What?" he asked.

"It's nice," she said. "But you really can't go up and down those stairs. Had we known at the hospital, we wouldn't have released you."

"You're joking."

"I'm not. This is an unfit living situation for someone in your condition."

"Are you going to report that?" Tanner's chest tightened. He didn't want to displace his friends—he wouldn't. And he didn't want them to feel bad either.

"I have to, Tanner."

"I liked that third place the most," he said. "I'll buy it tomorrow."

"You can't just buy a house in one day."

Tanner frowned. He didn't actually know what it took to buy a house. "What about an apartment then? There's got to be something open for immediate occupancy."

"I'll look when I get home. Because Doctor Brady won't like this." She faced him. "I'm sorry. I'm not trying to make trouble."

He grinned. "Yes, you are. You're a troublemaker." His hands seemed to have a mind of their own as they slid around her waist. She leaned slightly into him, barely putting any pressure or weight on his injured ribs. She took a deep breath of him, which caused a rush of satisfaction to pour through him. All too soon, and before he could kiss her, she stepped out of his embrace. "I'll call you later, okay? I need a plan for Doctor Brady."

"Okay." He watched her go, pure exhaustion filling him as soon as she disappeared upstairs.

She called but he was asleep. When he woke near ten o'clock, he didn't dare return her call. She said she'd be up for work by five, and he didn't want to cause her to lose sleep. She'd found him an apartment—had even gone so far as to call the landlord and line up a showing for tomorrow afternoon. Summer thought he'd like it, and she'd texted him a link.

The pictures looked great. New paint, new carpet, new countertops. A one-bedroom place on the first floor of an apartment building near downtown. It was for rent right now, but he noticed the rent-to-own label near the bottom of the listing.

He slept a lot the next day but managed to get his physical therapy done before Summer arrived. They looked at the apartment, and he put a deposit and the first month's rent down on it. He could move in that night if he wanted to.

As he slid into the booth at the diner, he exhaled heavily. "There's just one more problem," he said to Summer as she picked up her menu.

"What's that?"

"I don't actually have a bed, or a couch, or anything to put in that apartment."

She met his eye with a glint of excitement in hers. "Are you saying you need to go shopping? Because I happen to be a professional shopper."

"You also happen to have a tiring, full-time job." He ordered a soda and a plate of nachos when the waitress stopped by. Summer opted for water and an extra plate so she could share his nachos.

"Tomorrow is my day off." She leaned her elbows on the table and leaned into them. "So I can get you a bed, a couch, a kitchen table, anything you want."

"I don't *want* any of it."

She flinched at his words, and he realized how they sounded. "I just mean I don't want you to have to deal with it."

She relaxed and extended her hands across the table for him to take. "I don't mind."

"It doesn't feel like something my girlfriend would do, and yet I hate that you're not my girlfriend."

"I'm not?"

"Not until that fifth date kiss." He smirked at her and glanced up as the waitress approached. He released her hands to make room for the food, and he watched her for any signs of resistance to actually being his girlfriend.

She ate for a few minutes, and he liked the fact that they could exist in silence and still be comfortable. She shattered that peace when she asked, "So you don't count someone as your girlfriend until you kiss them?"

He almost choked on a sharp edge of a tortilla chip. "Not usually."

"So what date is this?"

"Number two," he said, enjoying her discomfort a little bit too much. "And you're the one who set the five-date rule, if you'll remember."

"I still don't see why I can't buy your furniture for you."

He couldn't quite figure it out in his head either. He took a few seconds to think, to take another drink, eat another nacho. "I don't want you to do it because it's your job."

"It *is* my job."

"But I don't want it to be."

She frowned, trying to understand. He found her attractive, so attractive that she was genuinely attempting to understand his point of view.

"It feels like a job for a girlfriend," he explained. "Or a best friend."

She leaned back, comprehension dawning in her eyes. "And I'm neither."

"Yet," he said quickly.

She lifted her glass to her lips and drank. "So you don't want me to do it?"

He sighed, glad when the waitress arrived to take their dinner order. By the time she left, he'd ordered his thoughts. "I do want you to do it, yes. I just don't want you to feel like you have to do it because it's your job."

"I don't."

"Great."

Her lips twitched, but her expression remained serious. "All right, then. Great. Yeah." Her face bloomed with a smile—his favorite smile, the one that carried such light and warmth. The smile that opened a window right into her soul. "So let's talk color scheme."

Tanner groaned, the evening going downhill with just a few words.

The following Sunday, Tanner woke in his new apartment. His new bed the best Three Rivers had to offer. His new couch had been the perfect place to hold Summer as they watched a movie on date four. Date four, which was last night. Date four, which had been take-out at his place, with a movie after. She'd fallen asleep, and he'd held her against his side, listening to her breathe in and out, feeling her chest rise and fall against him, falling a little more for her.

On Wednesday evening, he'd gone out to Three Rivers Ranch to see his horse, but he hadn't been able to stay for long. Seeing Ethan and Brynn working with all those horses, smelling the hay and dirt and fresh air, watching the activity of the cowboys, the animals, the horses, and he just couldn't. Grief overwhelmed him, and he'd retreated to the cab of Ethan's truck after only a few minutes.

Date three had happened on Thursday night. He'd asked her for something quiet they could do together, and she'd suggested a movie. He'd enjoyed the popcorn, the soda, the company. Oh, the company. Every minute he spent with Summer he fell a little more. It was a new and strange sensation, one he'd never truly experienced before. One he wasn't even sure was happening for real. One that scared him into slowing down.

He got out of bed and got ready for church. Summer was stopping by to pick him up, though he could walk there as part of his physical therapy. She'd claimed there was no way he could walk four blocks in the mid-July heat.

"In *Texas*," she'd emphasized, as if he'd never been to the south before. He'd smiled and said he'd love a ride. What he really wanted was to be at her side. Hold her hand. Get to know more about her.

He'd heard about her two older brothers, where she'd gone to nursing school, all about her history in Three Rivers. The only thing they hadn't spent much time discussing was their past relationships.

Tanner had stuck to his family, the death of his father, his rodeo career, his horses, and his childhood. That pretty much encapsulated his life—if he didn't detail the women he'd dated over the past dozen years. He didn't even want to remember them that much, and he couldn't imagine telling someone as innocent and wonderful as Summer about them.

"You'll have to tell her eventually," he muttered to himself as he pulled a necktie over his head. His mother had sent a box of clothes to Ethan's, and another was on its way to his new apartment. He'd sent Summer with his credit card, and she'd gone all out. Bathroom towels, shower curtain, coffee maker, kitchen utensils, a big-screen television, the works. Various stores had been delivering goods for days, and she'd promised him last night that it wasn't over yet.

His phone sounded, and he saw Summer's name flash on the screen. His heart leapt to the back of his throat for no reason he could name. That right there was something new that had never happened with another woman. He'd been excited to see some of them, sure. But never in this giddy, heart-galloping kind of way. Never in a way that made him smile before he even saw them. Never in a way that made him worry about what he might do or say to drive them away.

Because, in the past, he'd always known he'd drive them away. He was Tanner Wolf, and women came to him, not the other way around. He didn't sacrifice to be with anyone, not even his family. A pang of regret lanced through him. He'd felt it many times over the past year, and yet he hadn't managed to give up the rodeo.

As if he'd been hit with a freeze-ray, understanding streamed into his mind. He couldn't give up the rodeo. Hadn't been able to, though he'd felt guilty about leaving his aging mother alone in Colorado and he hadn't yet met his new nephew.

"Is that why I got hurt?" he asked his reflection, really directing the question to God. He hadn't understood Ethan's statement about being lucky to be here in Three Rivers. But maybe he did now. He *was* lucky to be so near to his friends when he needed them most. Suddenly, the very thought of returning to the circuit, even for team roping, tasted like poison.

Meeting Summer Hamblin certainly had been the best thing that had happened to him since he'd tried to live a clean life.

Are you coming? his phone flashed again. Another text from Summer. *Do you need help?*

"Coming," he dictated into the speaker, hit send, and pulled on his left boot. He could spend the sermon in introspection and he didn't want to make her late because he couldn't get outside his own head.

CHAPTER EIGHT

Summer snuggled into Tanner's side as much as she dared. Number one, the church in Three Rivers was the second biggest hotbed of gossip. All the older ladies saw who came with whom and they discussed everything—and everyone—under the sun at the salon, the number one place for gossip.

Number two, she didn't want to put more pressure on Tanner's ribs. He kept his hand on her bicep, kept her close, as Pastor Scott talked about forgiveness. Summer had heard countless lectures on forgiving others over the years, but the pastor wasn't talking about that today. No, he was talking about forgiving oneself.

Summer had a considerably harder time with that topic, and though the delectable smell of Tanner's cologne and the heat of his touch threatened to steal her attention, she focused on the sermon.

Not that she'd done anything terribly wrong in her life.

Nothing she felt gut-wrenching guilt over. But she hadn't fully addressed her issues with making smart decisions when it came to men. She'd been blaming herself for years about Drew's wandering eye. If she were as pretty as Victoria. As funny as Victoria. As attentive to Drew's needs as Victoria.

She'd been angry and hurt at both of them, but somehow, through the lectures and sermons, she'd forgiven them. Herself? Not so much.

Maybe that's why you don't go on second dates, she thought. *Didn't,* she amended. Because she'd certainly been out with Tanner more than once. Four times, to be exact, and she was hoping tonight would count as number five so he'd finally kiss her.

The thought of becoming his girlfriend, of kissing him, sent her into a tailspin. She liked him a lot. Enjoyed spending time with him, was interested in learning more about his life and who he was, what made him tick. Their conversations had been lively and without awkward silences. She had every right to be attracted to him. He was a cowboy with manners, after all.

At the same time, she still didn't trust herself to make a wise choice when it came to men. Maybe a relationship with Tanner was futile. Would he really stay in Three Rivers? Maybe his kindness and his willingness to share his life stories with her were all for show. Or maybe they weren't. She wasn't sure, and therein lay the problem.

The sermon ended, and Tanner stood to sing the final hymn. He balanced his weight on his good leg, one hand gripping the pew in front of him for extra support. He had terrible pitch but sang right along as if he was in key. Summer grinned and kept her eyes on the hymnal so he wouldn't realize she was amused by his bad singing.

The song ended, but the chords hung in the rafters. Summer closed her eyes and listened to them, hoping for the whispers of angels to reverberate through the lingering notes. Peace filled her from head to sole, and she sighed with contentment.

"Are we eating with your parents tonight?" Tanner asked, his warm hand claiming hers.

"No, I thought we'd do something else."

"What'd you have in mind?"

She glanced at him as he shuffled down the row and into the aisle. "You've been talking a lot about your horses. I'd like to meet one of them."

He'd been nodding to a family, but he froze. "My horses?"

"You have one out at the ranch, don't you?"

His teeth clenched and his jaw jumped. "Yeah, I suppose I do."

"You suppose you do?" She tugged on his arm in an attempt to get him to look at her. "Why don't you want to go out to the ranch?"

"It's not that I don't want to."

She tilted her head and tried to read the tonalities in his voice. She couldn't quite make them line up, but he wore the same look now that he had when he was trying to explain about why he did and didn't want her to buy his furniture.

"I think it's exactly that you don't want to," she said.

"It's just that—" He exhaled and paused, letting several people stream past them toward the exit. "It's just that the ranch, and my horses, and seeing all those cowboys reminds me of what I don't have anymore."

Summer turned into him to make the aisle wider for Tim Barney as he approached in his wheelchair. "And what exactly don't you have anymore?"

Tanner waved his hand, an edge of unhappiness in his eyes Summer wanted to erase. "You know. Cowboy stuff."

She reached up and flicked the brim of his hat. "Seems like you have plenty of cowboy left in you. *Cowboy*."

He smiled, but it lacked the passion, the fire, the drive she'd come to expect from him. "I can't drive out there."

"I have a car."

"I'll have to call Brynn and see if we can pick up a key or something."

Summer held her head high and moved faster toward the exit. "I already have it."

Tanner emitted a sexy growl that coaxed a giggle from Summer's throat. "Seems like it's not really my choice then."

"Not really, no." She danced out of his reach, a smile cemented in place. "Come on," she said. "It's beautiful country out there, and we can walk and talk and...." She lifted her eyebrows. "Be alone. It'll be fun."

"Are we goin' right now?"

She feigned shock. "I'll need to change first. I can't wear these heels out on the ranch. I'd break my ankle, and well, you're in no shape to carry me back if that happens."

"I would try," he said, a smile finally forming on his face and crinkling those intoxicating eyes.

"I know you would." She linked her arm through his. "So I'll change real quick and then you can, and then maybe we can grab a bucket of fried chicken and head out. Sort of a private picnic on the prairie." She glanced down at his injured leg. "Will you be okay with the hard cast? You might get it off this week."

"I'll be fine." He pulled her close and pressed his lips to her forehead. "I like the private part of this proposal."

She did too, and she worked to calm the thundering of her heart. An hour later, she pulled into a spot in front of Brynn's training facility. They wandered down the dusty aisles until they arrived outside a stall where a tall, black horse hung his head over the wall.

"Hey, Gridiron." He stroked the horse's cheeks and down his neck. The horse pushed his nose into Tanner's chest and snuffled. "I know, boy. I know. Sorry." He whispered to the horse with reverence, as if Summer wasn't present. She felt awe as she watched him with his horse, a bond there she hadn't comprehended before.

"So this is Summer." Tanner stepped back to allow Summer to move to his side. "She's a skittish thing. Works with sick people and not animals. Can you believe that?"

Gridiron tossed his head like the idea of nursing was

absolutely ludicrous. Summer reached out and stroked her hand down his nose. "Hey, boy."

They fed him an apple and Tanner turned to her. "So you've met him. And I'm starving."

"Okay, picnic then. You get to carry the blanket. I'll bring the food." They returned to her car and gathered everything before Tanner set his feet west, away from the barns, the dual homesteads, the entire ranch. Summer let him, because it seemed like there were phantoms in the horse stalls, ghosts in the barns, apparitions around the ranch she didn't understand.

"The wind says things out here, doesn't it?" She turned her face into the breeze and closed her eyes. "My granddaddy used to tell me they were angels, taking notes of all I did and whispering to me to do better."

She opened her eyes and smiled at him. "I liked thinking I had angels around me, especially when he told me he would be one of them once he died."

"Were you close to your grandparents?"

"Yeah, they lived right next door to us. You?"

"Only my dad's parents. My mom grew up in Maine, and we never went there. Hardly knew them."

They reached a stand of trees, and Summer took the blanket from Tanner and spread it on the ground. She knelt on one corner and put the food in the middle. It took Tanner several seconds to lower himself to the ground, and he groaned when he did. "I might be sleepin' here tonight," he said. "Not sure I'll be able to get up."

"I'll help you."

"I weigh three times what you do."

"Three times?" She scoffed. "I think your muscles have gone to your head." She reached for a container of mashed potatoes, but Tanner swept her hand up in his, bringing her fingers to his lips.

"I think this is date number five," he murmured. "Isn't it?"

According to Belinda, it was actually number thirteen, but Summer didn't tell Tanner that. She simply eased into his arms, going slow so he could adjust into a comfortable position. He cradled her close, the admiration and desire evident in his expression.

"Well?" he asked. "Is it?"

"It is," she confirmed.

"Thank goodness." Tanner leaned down and captured her lips with his. He kissed her in a way she'd never been kissed before. His touch held passion yet restraint. Excitement yet patience. "I've been dyin' to do that," he whispered, his smile curving against her lips. He kissed her again, this time drawing her deeper, exploring longer, leaving her dizzy when he finally pulled away.

"Worth dyin' for?" she asked in a timid tone, the taste of his mouth still in hers. Tanner had a special way of making her feel beautiful, something she'd never really felt before. He *told* her she was beautiful every time he saw her—and she was starting to believe it.

"Definitely." He touched his lips to her neck, her jaw, and finally her lips again. She could kiss this man all day and all night and never grow weary of it. His feelings streamed from him, and she released hers too.

"I'm falling for you," he whispered against her earlobe before touching his lips there.

She gripped his shoulders tighter and brought her eyes level with his. "Is that okay?"

"Of course it's okay." He searched her expression. "Is it okay with you?"

She grinned, nodded, and said, "I'm falling for you too. And you know what? My friend says this is actually our thirteenth date." She giggled. "But she's been counting me walking with you over to your physical therapy appointments and stuff like that."

"Lucky number thirteen," he murmured before kissing her again.

CHAPTER NINE

Tanner couldn't believe the difference between kissing Summer and kissing the other women he had. But there was a marked difference. This relationship felt real—something none of his others had.

"Summer," he murmured sleepily. They'd eaten and kissed some more. Now they lay in each other's arms, the summer breeze drifting lazily over them, keeping them cool enough.

"Yeah?"

"I've been thinking about something."

"Oh yeah?"

"Yeah." He sighed. "I don't think you'll like it."

That got her attention and she lifted her head to look at him. "What is it?"

"Well, my mom is getting older. I only have one brother, and he just had his third son. I haven't even met the baby yet."

She watched him, those compassionate eyes waiting. He sighed and gazed into the sky so he could say his next words. "I know I said I was going to stay in Three Rivers, but I think I need to return to Colorado Springs." He turned his eyes on her so he could see her reaction.

She blinked and opened her mouth to say something. Nothing came out.

"Not right away," he added. "I committed to the eight weeks of homecare. I'm going to do that. But when the doctor says I can travel, I'm going to have to get back up to Colorado Springs." His voice drifted quieter with each word. "I have a house there. My brother and his family live there. My mom needs help from time to time."

The sky seemed full of golden light, and he appreciated it. He couldn't remember the last time he'd stopped to appreciate nature. He was busy, traveling, riding, roping, winning.

"I think maybe God allowed me to get injured so I'd slow down," he said, each word weighed and measured before he spoke it. "So I could be part of my family's life. So I wouldn't miss too much time with them." He stopped speaking, everything inside him, everything he'd been thinking about since that morning, finally out.

He wanted her to say something, but she remained silent. She settled back into the crook of his arm, her head on his chest, but her body felt stiff next to his.

"What do you think?" he asked.

"I don't know," she said. "It's not my life." She didn't

sound angry or upset. She didn't sound non-committal either.

Tanner wasn't sure how to read her. "I—"

"Maybe now isn't a great time for us to be starting a relationship," she said.

"That isn't what I meant."

She exhaled and sat up. He envied her for how easy it was. He couldn't even take a deep breath. "My life is in Three Rivers," she said. "I have a good job here. Friends. My parents."

"I know." He tried to sit too, but his ribs protested. He lay back down, that beautiful sky above him in direct contrast to the conversation before him. "I'm not saying you have to move."

"Then there can't be a relationship." She shook her head, her honeyed curls bouncing against her shoulders. He couldn't see her face as she set about cleaning up their picnic. "I'd like to get home. I have to work early in the morning."

"Summer," he said.

She twisted back to him. "I don't understand. You know what? It's okay. But this is why I don't go on second dates." She grabbed the bag of trash she'd collected in one hand, stood, and reached for the bucket of fried chicken. "Will you bring the blanket, please? I'll see you at the car."

"Wait," he called, but she didn't slow or turn around. She wasn't walking particularly fast, but seeing as Tanner wasn't sure how he was even going to regain his feet, he'd never catch her. "What does this have to do with going on second dates?" he yelled.

She acted like she hadn't heard him. Maybe she hadn't. Tanner rolled onto his side, and then his stomach, where he only stayed for a second before pushing himself onto his hands and one knee. Standing from there took effort and caused some pain, but he managed to get on his feet. He rested one palm against the tree trunk while he caught his breath.

Foolishness flowed through him, hot and strong. What a terrible time to tell a woman he'd be leaving town in seven weeks. Why had he done that right after spending an afternoon kissing her? He cursed his stupidity as he folded the blanket.

With every step back to the ranch road where she'd parked, he asked the Lord to help him set things right. Nothing came to mind, but Tanner wasn't particularly well-versed in hearing the voice of the Lord, so he didn't have much to go on when he arrived at Summer's car.

She wasn't there, and his eyes flew around the ranch. There was Squire Ackerman's homestead, with its sprawling, green lawn. Pete Marshall's homestead faced it, with a much smaller lawn. The Courage Reins facility sported windows that gleamed in the sunlight. The parking lot was empty, but the ranch road that ran between the barns and the facility held lots of trucks.

Brynn's boarding stable seemed empty as well, and Tanner could only see a lone cowboy making his way from the chicken coops down the road. He disappeared from sight behind the Courage Reins building, leaving Tanner alone in the wilderness.

He'd felt that way for a while. Traveling and performing had him constantly surrounded by people yet always by himself. He'd never been lonely until this year, and he'd felt even more secluded from society since his injury.

The door to the boarding stable knocked against the frame, drawing his attention there. He tossed the blanket on the roof of the car and limped over to the swinging door and went inside the stable, knowing Summer had relocked it after they'd visited Gridiron. She had to be there.

Sure enough, he saw her silhouette down the aisle by the horse. He approached slowly, his tongue thick in his mouth. "Summer," he said. "I don't know what to do with my life. God hasn't told me that yet. It could be that I live here and just go to Colorado Springs often."

She turned her face toward him, but with the sunlight streaming in behind her, he couldn't read her expression.

"Please talk to me," he said. Getting a woman to talk was usually not a problem. But he'd learned that everything with Summer was different, though he had known her to fill conversations with just her voice. "What does going on a second date have to do with this?"

She shook her head, a strangled sound coming from her throat. It was part laugh and part sob. Tanner reached her and drew her into his arms. "I didn't mean to upset you. I just wanted to share with you what I'd been thinking about. What I'd felt at church today." He smoothed her hair down and pressed his lips to her temple. "I'm really sorry. It was stupid timing. I shouldn't have said anything."

Several seconds passed before she released her hold on his back and inched away. She looked up at him. "I'm glad you told me," she said. "I want you to be comfortable telling me things. I just...." She shook her head and looked back at the horse. "I don't go on second dates, because then I can't have a relationship. And then I don't have to feel like this when it ends."

"It doesn't have to end," Tanner said. "I'm just thinking out loud. I haven't even spoken to my mother yet." But Tanner knew she'd be thrilled to have him closer to home. "I don't even know what I'd do for a job."

"You could train horses," Summer said.

"Yeah, sure." Tanner loved working with horses, but the end goal—winning—had always kept his focus where it needed to be. Would training them for someone else be enough? He wasn't sure. "And I can do that here or in Colorado Springs, or anywhere else I want." He brushed his fingers down the side of her face. "Tell me I didn't ruin everything."

The slightest curve bent her lips. She nudged his shoulder. "You didn't ruin everything."

Relief spread through him like wildfire, consuming all his anxiety and fear. "I'm not very good at this dating thing," he admitted. "I don't really know what I'm doing."

She stepped out of his arms and laced her fingers

through his. They took lazy steps toward the exit, every other one of his stuttered as he leaned into the crutch. "Surely you knew a lot of women on the rodeo circuit. You're a big celebrity."

His throat turned dry. "Yeah," he said. "There wasn't a shortage of women. But I didn't really date any of them." He cleared his throat. "What about you? When was your last second date?" He couldn't believe the cowboys in this town hadn't snatched someone like Summer right up. She was the epitome of Southern beauty, Southern charm, Southern manners.

"Uh, it's been a while."

"Serious boyfriends before that?"

"A couple." She took a deep breath. "They're the reason I instated the no second date rule. Every relationship I was in ended in disaster. Usually with my heart in pieces on the floor." She lifted one shoulder in a shrug. "I don't want to get hurt like that again. So it was easier to just stop dating."

He squeezed her hand. "I can't believe you didn't have men asking."

"Believe it."

"I don't. Surely you just told them no."

"All right, fine. I used my job as an excuse for why I couldn't go out with them. Too busy. Although." She paused in the doorway and pointed at him. "There were some that weren't interested in going out with *me* again."

He growled and pressed her into the doorframe. "I can't even fathom that." He traced his lips down the side of her face, claiming her lips in the sweetest kiss he'd experienced in his life. "Maybe it was just my luck," he whispered. "To meet you in the hospital, where you couldn't make up an excuse not to see me."

"Maybe," she said breathlessly before pulling his face closer for another kiss.

TANNER CONTINUED TO WRESTLE WITH HIS decisions. He wasn't sure what was right, what he wanted, what God wanted, or who to believe. He didn't have a great track record of making decisions, so he sat back and waited for someone else to tell him what to do.

But that wasn't really working out either. He didn't want to do what Ethan thought he should. Wasn't interested in listening to his brother guilt him into doing something he didn't truly want to do. And God was absolutely silent on the subject, though Tanner spent hours on his knees over the next couple of weeks.

Frustrated at his lack of personal progress, he pushed himself physically. He improved immensely, and his appointment with Dr. Verdad proved it.

"Your leg is healing nicely," he said. "Even your ribs seem to be on the mend much faster than I thought they'd be. Any shortness of breath?" He pushed aside Tanner's shirt to examine the bruises the bull had left behind.

"Yeah, sure," Tanner said. "Usually only when I'm

walking though. During my physical therapy. Otherwise, it's gotten way easier to breathe."

"The bruises are nearly gone."

"My mother sent me some lavender and tea tree oil for them. She'll be thrilled to know it worked." Tanner chuckled, and it didn't hurt nearly as much as it had previously. "I'll be glad to stop rubbing myself down every night."

Dr. Verdad smiled with him, but Tanner thought it might have actually been a frown. He grinned to himself and made a note to tell Summer about the non-smile. She'd said she and one of her nursing friends weren't sure if Dr. Verdad's smiles could actually be categorized as such.

"That cast can come off now, and we'll put you in a walking brace."

Tanner's hopes soared. "That's great," he said, keeping his voice even.

"Let's double your steps," he said. "Who's your home-care nurse?" He flipped some pages.

"Summer Hamblin," Tanner said. "She's been coming regularly."

"Since you can't drive, and she works at the hospital full-time, it might be tricky to get you over here."

"I can manage. My apartment's only a few blocks from here. I don't need to drive."

Dr. Verdad flipped through some more pages. "Twice more per week. Let's do Monday and Thursday." He scribbled something on the chart and slapped it on the counter. "Anything else concerning you?"

Tanner couldn't think of anything, so the appointment ended. He couldn't wait to get the cast off. Couldn't wait to start living his life again. Couldn't wait to see Summer.

She sat on the lawn outside his apartment building when he came hobbling up. "Hey," he said. "How long you been here?"

"About five minutes." She fanned herself with a folded piece of paper. "I'm about to melt."

He laughed and swept her into a kiss hello. "Well, c'mon in where there's air conditioning." He told her about his doctor's appointment, and they walked a few blocks to a fast-casual place where he got a burrito and she ordered a taco salad.

Tanner could see himself doing this every evening, and not just in the summer when the days stretched until ten p.m. But every day, every night. He wanted to see Summer, feel Summer, kiss Summer every evening when she got off work. He wanted to hear her laugh the way she did when he did his rodeo announcer impression. He wanted to walk back to *their* apartment, holding her hand.

With perfect clarity, Tanner knew he'd fallen hard for Summer. He kissed her under the rising moon, pulling back when he could hardly breathe.

"You okay?" she whispered.

"Absolutely okay."

She gave him a peculiar look, tucked her hair behind her ear, and said she'd see him tomorrow.

With his feelings for her clear to him, he worked on

getting other areas of his life in order. He called his mother every week. He touched base with his brother.

With only two weeks until his eight-week homecare would end—two weeks until he could potentially leave town—he called Ethan.

"I think I'm ready," he told the other cowboy. "When can I hitch a ride with you out to Courage Reins?"

"You're sure?" Ethan had been reminding Tanner about the therapeutic riding center every chance he got.

Tanner took a deep breath and it only stretched his chest too far at the very end. "I'm sure. I can't get on a horse yet. Doctor Verdad said just because I'm in a walking cast doesn't mean I'm all the way healed. But I can walk next to a horse or something."

"I'll talk to Pete tomorrow. Get something set up for you."

"Great." Tanner hung up, feeling grateful and grounded for the first time since the rodeo.

CHAPTER TEN

Summer stared at her computer screen, the memory of Tanner's last kiss on her mind and lingering on her lips. Something had changed. He'd never kissed her like that before. They hadn't spoken much about his plans in recent weeks. He'd finally admitted he didn't have any plans, that he didn't know what to do.

She'd been trying to live one day at a time, enjoy every moment with him. And she had. Problem was, if he chose to leave Three Rivers, he'd leave a hole in her life the size of a barge. Every night after she returned home, she questioned herself. Had she made another erroneous decision by getting involved with Tanner? Why couldn't she just fall in love with a local cowboy? Or the deli owner. Or someone who didn't have a completely separate life in a city hundreds of miles away.

She'd asked him if he was okay, and he seemed okay. But that kiss…. Her fingers drifted to her lips, and she startled when she touched them. She shut down her Internet browser and padded down the hall to her bedroom. She should've gone to bed an hour ago, yet Tanner had dominated her thoughts so completely, she hadn't.

With only two weeks until his homecare ended, Summer wished he had a plan. Wished his plan included her. But they'd only been dating officially for five weeks; she'd only known him for seven. But he carried so much strength in his person, he commanded a room when he entered it.

She understood easily how he'd dominated the rodeo circuit, why women—why everyone—gravitated toward him. He'd been surprisingly soft-spoken, but she'd learned over the past several weeks that he hadn't always been that way. That just about a year ago he'd decided to make a change in his life. Make room for God in his life.

If anything, learning that about him had made him more attractive to Summer. "Like you need another reason to fall in love with him," she muttered as she climbed into bed. She froze, every muscle in her body seizing.

Was she in love with Tanner Wolf?

She blinked, blinked. She'd been in love with one other man in her life. Drew. And it felt a lot like this.

Her muscles turned spongy and she collapsed onto her back, a smile spreading from one side of her face to the other.

You are in love with him, she thought as a giggle leaked from her lips. At the same time as her euphoria, a sense of dread settled over her. She'd gone and fallen in love with a man who might not even be in town next month.

She rolled onto her side, her eyes staring into the darkness. She'd be strong like Tanner was. Whatever the next several weeks held, she'd be glad she had this brief time with him.

"Thank you," she whispered into the blackness, to the Lord. "Thank you for letting me love again."

Over the course of the next week, Tanner kept putting her off. He cancelled all their usual evening appointments for physical therapy, and that meant all of their dinners and subsequent good-night kisses.

Finally, Summer had had enough. She called Tanner, who answered on the second ring. "Hey, there," he said with a smile in his voice.

"Hey, yourself," she said, the frustration she felt coming through in her tone. "Where are you?"

"I'm, uh…."

She stood on the lawn of his apartment, and she knew he wasn't home.

"I'm, well, I'm out at the ranch."

Her eyebrows shot toward her hairline. "The ranch?" Based on the only time she'd taken him out there, she was surprised he'd return. He hadn't seemed keen on sticking around, and he'd confessed that the ranch symbolized everything he'd lost. "What are you doing out there?"

"Remember how I told you Ethan kept badgering me about the equine therapy program?"

"Hey!" another man said somewhere on Tanner's end of the line. "I did not *badger* you."

Tanner chuckled. "Well, I finally decided to take him up on his *offer*."

"Oh, so you've been ditching me every night this week for a horse."

"Several horses," Tanner said. "I work with a different one each night. They all kinda like me."

"Of course they do," she said dryly. She turned her back to his front door like someone might have their ear pressed to the wood to eavesdrop. "Why didn't you tell me you were going out to the ranch?"

"It was...." His voice dropped. "Something I was working through on my own."

She couldn't even begin to understand what Tanner had gone through emotionally when he'd lost the rodeo. It was his career. His livelihood. His entire world. She hadn't seen him experience anger, or remorse, or grief. But maybe he'd been suppressing it all this time.

A new, terrifying thought entered her mind. "You're not *riding* a horse, are you?"

"No, ma'am." He laughed. "Thank you, Nurse Hamblin, for checking up on me."

"Hey, someone has to."

"Where are you now?"

She hurried away from his building. "Just walking downtown." It was almost true. Another block or two and she'd be downtown. "Wondering if I'd have to eat dinner alone again."

"I'm real sorry, sweetheart. Ethan's just taking me out to the ranch now. I'll be a couple hours."

Now that she knew what he was doing, she didn't mind. "It's okay."

"I do need to talk to you later," he said. "Maybe I can have Ethan drop me off at your place?"

Her throat narrowed. What did he want to talk about?

"Summer?"

"My place is fine," she blurted before she could lose her confidence. "See you in a couple of hours."

Summer paced for most of those two hours, her overworked mind conjuring up every possible scenario. By the time Tanner knocked and pushed his way into her living room, she felt near tears.

He grinned, gathered her close, gave her a sweet kiss hello. His warm hands cupped the back of her neck and he breathed her in deep, deep. "I missed you."

Everything inside her calmed. She wrapped her arms around him and held on.

"One more week," he said, drawing himself away from her.

She eyed him. "Yeah. You don't think you'll need to enroll in further homecare?"

"I don't think so, no. Doctor Verdad said I can take off the walking cast if my leg feels strong enough, and I can do the strengthening exercises on my own." He kept his cowboy hat tipped down and she couldn't see his eyes.

"So I guess you'll be cleared to travel."

"I expect to be, yes."

"And you're going back to Colorado Springs." She wasn't even attempting to make her voice sound like a question.

He lifted his eyes to hers, and she saw something new in them. New, and unidentifiable. At least before he looked away. "Yes, Summer. I'm going to go back to Colorado Springs for a little while. Maybe a week. Maybe two. I was hoping—" His voice cracked and he cleared his throat. He took a step toward her and one away.

He drew a breath and looked right at her. Everything between them fell away, leaving her feeling exposed and vulnerable. He looked every bit as unmasked as she felt. "I was hoping you'd come with me. Meet my mother as my girlfriend. Stay at my house—it's plenty big for both of us. Nothing funny, I swear. Go meet my new nephew with me. That sort of thing."

Surprise shot through her. "You want—you want me to go with you?"

"If you can get the time off."

Summer didn't have untold millions sitting in a bank account somewhere. Taking a week off work was probably doable. She had enough vacation days for that. "I'll see what I can do when I get to work in the morning."

A smile split his face. "What do you think the chances are?"

"I don't know. Depends on how many other people have put in to have the time off."

He swept toward her with that power she admired about him, broken leg and all. "I really want you to come."

"I'll be sure to put that on my vacation request." She laughed as he caught her in his arms. "Doctor Brady should appreciate that."

Tanner sobered, his eyes taking on that super-serious edge they did sometimes. "I really want you to come," he said again. "Because I'm in love with you."

Summer sucked in a breath, hardly believing her ears. Tanner watched her with warmth in his eyes and those large hands holding her against his chest. "Tanner—"

"I know it's fast," he said. "But hey, I'm kind of a fast guy. When I figure out what I want, I go for it." He gave her half a grin, but it carried some nervous energy.

"What do you want?" she asked. "With your life, I mean."

"Still working that part out. But I do know I want you in it for a good, long while." His face softened. The edge in his eye melted. He dipped his mouth closer to hers, and when he kissed her, she realized what was different. What had been different in his touch.

He loved her.

CHAPTER ELEVEN

"I can't get work off." Summer sniffed as if she'd been crying. "Three nurses already put in for time off, and—"

Tanner swung his legs over the side of the couch and rubbed the back of his head. "Let's go a different week then."

"No." Her voice definitely sounded nasally. Choked up. Tanner started looking for his boots so he could go see her. "You go without me. I'll go next time. This way, you'll be able to stay as long as you want. Might be better anyway."

"It won't be better," he said. "I can wait. My mom isn't going anywhere." He'd need to make all his phone calls again, but he could. He didn't want to make the six-hour drive without Summer. The very thought sounded like torture. He'd told her he loved her, and he'd never felt something so deep, so pure. He'd never felt so free.

She hadn't said it back, but everything in her eyes, everything in her touch, testified that she loved him too. He'd have to trust those feelings for now. Sure, it was a fast relationship, but like he'd said, when he knew what he wanted, he did it. It was getting to that point that seemed to take time.

Summer was a passionate woman too. She could fall in love quickly, he knew. Women like her often did, which was why he didn't want to go to Colorado Springs without her. He wouldn't hurt her if he could help it.

She'd started talking, and he hadn't heard all of it. But he heard her when she said, "You should just go."

Tanner didn't know what to do. He didn't know what she wanted him to say, what she really wanted him to do. He pressed his eyes closed and offered up a prayer requesting help. He'd felt like he needed to get home to visit as soon as possible.

"When can you get off?" he asked.

"Not until almost Halloween."

Tanner's heart sank, taking his hopes with it. "It's only the beginning of September."

"Margie has a daughter getting married. Belinda wants her baby's first birthday off. Jean always goes to Jamaica in the fall." She sounded crestfallen, but determined too. "You just go," she said. "You'll call me every night and tell me about your mom, and the baby, and your house."

Helplessness pushed against his every breath. "Okay," he said. "And we'll go near Halloween. Can you put in for the time off now?"

"I already did," she said.

"Great." He hung up and decided to get up and do his physical therapy. The week passed, and he got his cast off and his travel to Colorado okayed by Dr. Verdad. He packed and picked up his truck from Ethan's.

"So I'm set to leave in the morning," he said to Summer on Sunday evening. He ran his fingers through her hair. "I'll be gone a week or so."

"I know," she said sleepily. "I'm on swing shift, remember?"

"I remember." He smiled up at the stars. Now that he could get around easier, they'd been spending evenings in her backyard, where she had a hammock. "No calls before noon."

"Unless it's an emergency."

When it was time for him to go, he cupped her face in his hands, whispered, "I love you, Summer," and kissed her. It didn't feel like a final kiss to him, though she pulled away sooner than he liked. She smiled, but it held sadness. Sadness he wished he could erase. Sadness he never wanted to see in those blue eyes.

The next morning, the fall sky matched the color of Summer's eyes. He smiled into it and made sure to stop every two hours to get out and walk. His leg needed the extra circulation, and he disliked the weakness he felt in his knee. He made it to Colorado Springs without any problems.

His mother was working, so he went to his house first. Embarrassment squirreled through him when he pulled up to the gate and remembered it required a code to enter. What a different life he had here. He felt like a foreigner in his own life, pulling into his own garage. Four wide, each housed a different truck.

What would Summer think of that? he wondered as he glanced down the row of them. They all gleamed as if they'd just been washed. The garage floor was likewise spotless, and Tanner knew that the mansion he lived in would be equally clean. After all, he paid good money to keep it that way whether he was home or not.

Sure enough, Clarissa had been in recently. Tanner took in the vaulted ceilings and long, tiled halls. Again, he wasn't quite sure who lived here. Him, or a version of himself he no longer was. Gooseflesh broke out on his arms as an uncomfortable feeling descended on him.

He didn't belong here. Didn't belong in this house. All of this extravagance belonged to the Tanner Wolf of the past. The man he'd left behind somewhere between here and Three Rivers.

Suddenly, he craved the simplicity of Three Rivers. Of having one grocer, and a handful of choices for dinner, and a rusty old ranch truck to get around.

He pulled out his phone to text Summer, but paused with her name called up on his screen. He couldn't explain this to her. Horror that he'd almost brought her here snaked through him. He navigated out to his contacts and found Theo. He dialed that number as he crossed the house to the other side, where his master suite was.

"Tanner," Theo said. "It's been a long time."

"Theo," Tanner said. "I'm back in town. Wondering if you might be able to come over to the house sometime this week."

"Sure, what's up?"

"I want to sell my place," Tanner said.

"You want to…sell your place?"

"That's right."

"The place I spent a year looking for? The one that couldn't be within five miles to the freeway? The one that needed to have at least a half an acre of land? That house?"

Tanner cringed at his vainness. His *past* vainness. "Yes, Theo. That house. It doesn't…suit me anymore."

Theo laughed, the sound as dark and rich as freshly brewed coffee. "You said that house was perfect. And it was."

"I've changed," he said simply.

"I'll say you have." Theo exhaled. "So where will we be looking next? And if you say The Ranches, I'm hanging up."

Tanner scoffed at the idea of living on a fabricated ranch. "Even I haven't changed that much."

"Good. Because I can't stand the drive out there."

"Well, then you're probably really going to hate what I say next."

"I'm ready."

"I'm looking to buy something—something nice—in Three Rivers, Texas."

Once he'd convinced Theo that no, he was not joking, and yes, he wanted to relocate to the Texas panhandle as soon as possible, he showered and headed over to his mother's house. She pulled into the driveway just before him, and he swept her into a hug before she could even truly stand.

"Hey, Ma." He grinned down at her before he realized something was terribly wrong. A fist of ice punched him in his still-healing lungs. "What's wrong?"

"Kamry just called. Bill's been in a car accident."

Tanner's world sped and blurred. "An accident?" he managed to put through a too-tight throat. "Is he okay?"

"She said she didn't know. That we could come as soon as we could." She held up her phone. "I just hung up with her."

"Let's go." Tanner started for his truck, which he'd parked behind her car. They didn't speak on the way over, each lost in the last time they'd made a drive like this. They'd been separated then, connected only by a telephone call every so often as Tanner made his way home from Florida, where he'd been competing in one of the biggest rodeos in the country.

But his dad had just been in a car accident. He'd passed away before Tanner made it home.

Please, he prayed. Please let Bill be okay.

His mother rushed ahead of him into the hospital.

They found Kamry in the waiting room, alone. "Where are the boys?" his mother asked. "The baby?"

"They were all in the car with Bill." Her face bore splotches; her makeup had smudged around her eyes. "They won't tell me much of anything. They just keep saying a doctor will come out when there's something to tell."

Tanner didn't know what to do to comfort Kamry. He stepped up to her and encircled her in his arms. "It'll be okay," he whispered as she sagged into him. Then he prayed that he would be right.

An hour later, a doctor did come out to talk to Kamry. Everyone was alive, but they had various injuries. Only the baby had escaped unscathed because of the infant carrier. He took them back to see Bill and the two little boys, and with every step, Tanner felt his future changing.

How could he leave town next week? How could he leave them all and go back to Three Rivers? Back to traveling the rodeo circuit?

Bill needed his help right now, and in the coming months. Kamry would too. Tanner didn't believe for a single second that Bill's accident happening on the day Tanner arrived back in town was coincidence. No, God had brought him here to be a strength and support to his family.

And that was what he needed to do. Long-term.

CHAPTER TWELVE

Summer's stomach writhed with every minute that passed. Tanner hadn't texted her when he'd gotten to his house in Colorado Springs. That would've been hours ago. He hadn't called as she got off her shift. That was twenty minutes ago.

By morning, when she'd still heard nothing from him, she sent him a text—way before noon, as she'd had a hard time sleeping. He didn't respond.

She attacked her kitchen and bathroom with organic cleaning supplies, and an hour later, her house was the cleanest it'd been that year. Frustrated, with hours still until she needed to be at work, she called Belinda.

"Want to go to lunch?"

"Sure, I'm just finishing up with Oliver's bath."

"Is an hour okay?"

A splash sounded on Belinda's end of the line. "Should

be fine. I can take Ollie to daycare after that and we'll go to work together. Chinese?"

"Sure. See you then." But Summer couldn't stand to be inside her house, with her silent phone. So she pulled on a jacket, made sure she had everything she needed for work, and got in her car. She navigated to Tanner's apartment building and parked across the street. The Chinese restaurant was a couple of blocks away, and Summer walked the distance there.

A large park sat kitty-corner to the restaurant, and she stared through the trees that had started to lose their leaves. Mothers with small children enjoyed the fall sunshine, and Summer smiled at the innocence and carefree nature of the scene. If only her insides would stop churning like she'd swallowed a food processor.

She checked her phone. No texts. No calls. Not time for lunch. She sat on a bench and closed her eyes, letting the sound of the breeze, the calls of children, the rumble of traffic enter her soul.

Please let him call, she prayed. Surely the Lord had more important things to do than prompt a rodeo champion to call his girlfriend, but Summer couldn't help the plea. She believed God cared about her, cared about her life, as mundane as it may be.

Tanner didn't call. She got up and retraced her steps back to the Chinese restaurant. Belinda pulled in just as Summer stepped onto the curb, and she went to help her friend with her baby.

"I got his bag." She lifted the diaper bag out of the

backseat. Belinda thanked her as she unstrapped Oliver from the car seat. She straightened and met Summer's eye over the top of the sedan.

"What's wrong?"

Summer sighed. "What makes you think something's wrong?"

"You look like you haven't slept." Belinda came around the car. "You're out in public without mascara on."

Summer rolled her eyes. "I don't always wear mascara."

"Yes, you do. You even told Margie it was the only makeup that was essential to leave the house."

So maybe she'd said that. Once. A long time ago. She started toward the entrance. "Tanner went to Colorado Springs, right?"

"Right." Belinda spoke with caution.

"He was supposed to text me when he got there. Call me when I got off work. I haven't heard from him."

They entered the restaurant, where a small crowd of people had gathered for lunch. They joined the line before Belinda said, "You know what you should do? Go to Colorado Springs."

Summer reached for Oliver and took him from Belinda as a way to distract herself. "We've been over this. I can't get the time off."

"Tomorrow's your day off, right?"

"Right." Now Summer infused a bit of caution into her voice. Where was Belinda going with this? Did she really think Summer could get to Colorado Springs—a six-hour drive—and back in one day?

"So you leave in the morning. Meet up with him for lunch and dinner and breakfast, and come home the following day."

"I have to work that following day."

"So you'll call in sick. What will Doctor Brady do?"

"It'll make him short-staffed." Summer shook her head, dissatisfied with the plan. "I can't do that to him. It's not fair."

"He'll call around to the other nurses and see who can come in." Belinda nudged her. "And lucky you! I'll be available. I'll cover your shift." Belinda grinned like she'd just solved global warming or achieved world peace. She lifted her eyebrows, waiting. "So?"

Summer met her friend's eye with hope blooming, billowing, bouncing through her system. "But you hate working more than two days a week."

Belinda sobered, her dancing green eyes softening with compassion. "I'd do it for you."

Summer shrieked and wrapped her free arm around her friend. "Thank you, Belinda."

"Just one day, though," she said. "So you better not sleep in tomorrow like you do. You get up nice and early and hit the road." She smiled, the years of their friendship seeping between them. "Now, the real question is whether I should get the honey coconut shrimp or the sweet and sour chicken." She tipped her head back to study the menu.

"Should I call him?" Summer asked as she contemplated the menu too.

"Oh, make it a surprise," Belinda said just before stepping up to the counter and ordering the spicy peanut chicken.

SUMMER WORKED, AND SLEPT, AND GOT UP EARLY just like she'd promised. She packed an overnight bag, filled her car with gas, and queued up the map app on her phone. She didn't have his address, but she'd called Brynn Greene on her break the night before and gotten theirs.

She pulled into their driveway as the sun started to brighten the sky into yellows and golds. After knocking tentatively on the door, Brynn answered with Ethan coming out of the hallway behind her.

"Sorry it's so early," she said. "You could've texted me."

"Ethan was worried." Brynn glanced behind her, worry evident in the set of her mouth.

"I can't get ahold of anyone," he said. "Not his mom, his brother, him." He sighed. "Tanner's address and phone number are unlisted, obviously. I know he lives in a gated community somewhere. I managed to find his mom's address using her phone number." He handed her a slip of paper. "Summer, let us know what's goin' on, would you?"

She nodded as she absorbed the address written on the paper. "Do you think something's happened?"

"It's not like Tanner not to answer his phone," Ethan said. "Well, that's not true. It's totally like Tanner to ignore *my* calls. But yours?" He gazed at her with more wisdom in his eyes than she liked. She and Tanner had spent several evenings together with Brynn and Ethan. She'd become friends with them, but she wasn't sure how much Tanner had told his old rodeo pal.

"I'll let you know," she said, biting back the words she wanted to tell Ethan. She couldn't admit to him and Brynn that she loved Tanner. She hadn't even told him that yet, and he should be the first to know.

She put the address in her phone and headed north. Just under six hours later, the sun shone brightly overhead, though the temperature in the air hardly accounted for it. Colorado Springs seemed peaceful. A normal day in a normal city.

Easing into the driveway of the house where her map app had led her, she saw the garage door was open and a car was parked inside. That tricky hope rebounded from her gut to her throat and back.

She knocked and waited, rewarded when Tanner's mother opened the door. She looked a decade older than Summer remembered and she wore a pair of jeans and a jacket.

"Mrs. Wolf," she said. "I'm Summer Hamblin, the nurse who worked with your son, Tanner. Do you remember me?"

The woman blinked, recognition finally lighting her eyes. "Yes, of course. Are you looking for Tanner?"

Summer lifted her phone. "I can't seem to get ahold of him. I got your address from his friend, Ethan Greene."

The woman pulled the throat of her jacket closed and said, "Come in. It's cold outside."

Summer entered the house, sweeping it for signs of Tanner though she knew he had his own place in town. "Have you seen Tanner?"

"Yes, yes." She bustled into the kitchen. "He's at the hospital."

Alarm made Summer reach for the back of the couch to steady herself. "The hospital? Why's he at the hospital?"

"It's okay," his mother said. "Kamry is with him. She said she'd call if anything changed. I just couldn't sit there all day again today."

The interior of the house swam in darkness. Summer blinked, trying to clear her vision, trying to make the woman's words make sense. She was aware of Tanner's mother making tea and offering her some, but she sat on the couch—when had she sat on the couch?—and shook her head.

Tanner was in the hospital. Had been for a couple of days. And instead of calling *her*, he had someone named Kamry there with him. An in-town girlfriend?

Was she his out-of-town girlfriend?

Did he have a girlfriend in every city he visited?

She hated the distrustful feelings, the roaring envy, she felt rising through her, suffocating her. "I should go," she said as calmly as she could. She tested her weight on her legs and they held. "Thank you so much, Mrs. Wolf."

She escaped the house and had made it halfway down the sidewalk to her car when Mrs. Wolf called, "I just got a text," she said. "They went to The Red Door for lunch."

Summer turned and said, "Thanks," before hurrying to her car and backing out of the driveway as fast as she dared. She pulled over once a few blocks away and stared out the windshield.

Tanner went to lunch with Kamry? After being in the hospital?

"Nothing makes sense," she said. She flipped the car into drive. But she knew where she needed to go to get answers.

She pulled into the parking lot of The Red Door twenty minutes later. Her heart thundered in her chest, but she'd come this far.

Be brave, she told herself. She fisted her fingers, the anger she'd kept at bay surging now, and marched toward the entrance. The parking lot seemed fairly full for a weekday lunch crowd, and as soon as she entered, she knew she'd come to a ritzy, expensive establishment. Yellow lights hung above the tables and a man in a suit met her at the podium.

"Just one today, or is your party already here?"

"I'm—yes, I'm with Tanner Wolf."

The man scanned her, his gaze doubtful. "Mister Wolf didn't say he was expecting anyone else."

"Oh, he's not expecting me." Her fury and frustration seemed to double at the downward turn of the man's mouth. Past him, she spotted Tanner's trademark black cowboy hat. "There he is. I'll just go over and say hello."

She caught sight of a blonde woman just before the host stepped in front of her. "I can't let you do that."

Summer strained to see past him, to see who had replaced her in a matter of hours, who had made Tanner forget about her as soon as he'd gotten back into town. She couldn't see much, especially with the poor lighting. Her gut writhed. Maybe she had simply been Tanner's summer distraction. Someone to kiss until he could get back to his real life.

The thoughts felt traitorous and somewhat false, yet they burned all the same. She focused back on the man in her way. "Listen," she said. "I'm not going to make a scene." She darted around him and made her way closer to Tanner's table along the back wall. Halfway there, the host blocked her again, this time signaling to someone else.

Summer felt the weight of several pairs of eyes on her, and she swallowed. "I just want to talk to him for a second."

"Let me see if he wants to talk to you."

"Fine, you do that. He's my boyfriend, and I don't know who that other woman is." She stood on her tiptoes and managed to see that Tanner had finally looked in her direction. "I don't care who she is." She raised her voice, hoping it would carry to him. "He's *my* boyfriend!" She couldn't seem to get a proper breath, and by the time Tanner's much taller frame appeared behind the host, Summer's chest was heaving.

"It's okay, James. She is my girlfriend."

The world righted itself as Tanner smiled down at her. "What are you doin' here, Summer?" He embraced her, breathed in the scent of her hair, doing and saying all the right things. The exact right things she wanted him to.

She caught hold of reason and pushed him away. "You didn't text or call. You haven't answered your phone for two days. I had to get your mom's address from Ethan, and she told me you were in the hospital. But oh, it's okay, because *Kamry* was with you." She stabbed her finger to the blonde woman who'd come up behind Tanner.

They looked at each other, and Tanner started laughing. Kamry seemed stretched too thin, and Summer couldn't figure out why. Suddenly, she didn't want to figure out why.

She spun on her heel and marched out.

CHAPTER THIRTEEN

"You better go after her," Kamry said. "Tanner. Tanner, she's leaving."

Tanner's brain seemed several minutes behind. Kamry had pointed out that a woman was trying to get to him; he hadn't even noticed. Every cell in his body felt depleted as he'd only slept for a few hours since arriving in town.

He hadn't wanted to leave his brother's side. Hadn't wanted Kamry to have to shoulder the responsibility of caring for three injured family members. The boys would be released later that day, so he'd taken her to lunch for a little break. She'd go home with her kids and Tanner was planning to spend another night in the hospital with his brother.

Kamry filled his vision, her eyes tired yet earnest. "She left, Tanner. You should go after her. That was your Summer, right?"

His Summer.

Yes, she was his Summer. With his brain finally caught up, he strode forward, knocking into a nearby table he hadn't seen. He grunted against the pain and kept going. Bursting out of the door, he saw Summer in her car, tears tracking down her face.

He waved his arms and hobbled into the lot, a shout coming from his throat. She slammed on her brakes and their eyes met through the glass. He sucked in a breath, then another, as he watched her.

She sat back and put the car in park. He moved toward her window, which she rolled down halfway.

"Summer." He leaned against the car, his heart bobbing in his throat. "Come on back inside. Let's have lunch."

"I'm not hungry." She folded her arms.

"You would never stop for fast food," he said. "And it's only twelve-thirty, which means you haven't eaten since your dinner break last night." A smile crossed his face, but he erased it before she saw. She wouldn't like it. Didn't like it when he teased her, though he loved teasing her.

The opening in the window wasn't wide enough for him to bend through and kiss her. "Please," he tried. "We just barely started. You can officially meet my sister-in-law, and I'll tell you why I haven't even looked at my phone since I got here." He wasn't even sure where his phone was at the moment. He wasn't as attached to his devices as some people were, a mistake he realized now that his very worried girlfriend had driven six hours to make sure he was okay.

"Wait." Summer stared at him, her eyes bright and full of hope. Bright and full of anticipation. Bright and full of love. "Your sister-in-law?"

Tanner kicked a grin in her direction. "Yeah, Kamry is my sister-in-law. She's married to my brother, Bill. Remember? The only sibling I have?"

"I remember." Her voice sounded like she'd swallowed frogs. "I guess I better go park if I'm going to eat lunch."

"I guess you better." He fell back a few steps from the car, grateful she hadn't sped off with him standing in the parking lot. He followed her to an open spot and caught her as she stepped from the car. "I'm so glad you're here." Emotion coated his words and he swallowed to keep it down. He hadn't cried in years, but there were the tears burning behind his eyes.

He blinked, unsure of what was happening. He hadn't cried at his own injury. Hadn't cried when he'd seen Bill unconscious in that hospital bed. And here he was, weepy over a woman.

"I love you." He touched his lips to hers, glad when she responded in kind. "I'm so sorry I didn't call. I think my phone is in my truck. Or maybe my house. I'm not a hundred percent sure. It's probably dead by now too."

She clung to him, standing on her tiptoes, and swayed to music only she could hear. He smoothed his hands down her blouse and over her hips. "I don't see you in street clothes very often," he murmured. "You look nice."

She gave a choked laugh. "Anything's better than scrubs, right?" She lifted her eyes to his and he saw the fear, the hope, the desire within. "What happened, Tanner?"

Instead of telling her right away, he kissed her again, stealing from her strength, drawing from her determination. "Do you know how sexy it is that you drove here to see me?" He growled as he tracked his lips across her jaw and placed a kiss against the soft skin on her neck.

She sighed into him as she had in the past, and said, "Tanner, we're standing in a parking lot."

"Yeah." He kissed her again.

"Your sister-in-law is waiting."

"I told her all about you." He moved his mouth to her ear.

"I didn't want to tell you this in a parking lot."

"Tell me what?"

She ducked her head, effectively putting a couple of inches between their faces. "I'm in love with you," she said, her voice shaking at the end of the sentence. "That's why I drove six hours to find you. Because I love you." A shy smile slipped across her face. Her beautiful, freckly face he'd never get enough of.

He ran his thumb across her cheekbone. "Well, that's great news," he said before kissing her again. "In fact, that's the best news I've had this year."

She flinched away when he leaned forward to kiss her again. "Just this year?"

He laughed, the sound soaring into the sky. "My Summer sweetheart, it's the best news I've ever had in my whole life."

"I'M NOT GOING BACK TO THE RODEO," HE TOLD Summer later that night. Later, after their lunch with Kamry. Later, after they'd gotten the boys settled at home. Later, after he'd brought his mom for a visit with Bill, who was now awake. Later, after he'd taken his mother home, and checked on Bill, and thought he'd never be able to feel normal again. He thought he could sleep for days and still not feel normal.

She shifted in his arms. "You're not?"

His natural instinct was to hold her tighter, keep her close. So he did. She'd come home with him and not said a word about his gigantic house, the spotless nature of it, how sterile it felt. She'd been at his side all day, lending her strength and giving him comfort in the simplest ways like squeezing his hand and suggesting they get pizza for the boys and Kamry.

Now she lay against him on the couch. He wanted to go to bed, but he didn't want to leave her side.

"Tanner?"

He jerked out of his doze and took a moment to remember what they'd been talking about. "No. No more rodeo."

"But you love the rodeo."

"I do," he admitted. "But I know now that it's not my whole life. My family needs me. I need you."

She pressed her cheek to his chest again, completing

him, making him feel whole and alive. "What are you going to do?"

"I need to be here for a while," he said. "I'll keep the apartment in Three Rivers. If I send a credit card number with you, can you pay the rent for me?"

"Sure, but—"

"For a year," he said. "Then I'll have somewhere to stay when I come."

"How often will you come?"

"I don't know." A wave of exhaustion rolled over him. "As much as I can, sweetheart, okay? As much as I can." He'd told her about Bill's broken leg, his blood clotting issues. And Kamry had two little boys to tend to. One with a broken arm, one with minor cuts and bruises. Not to mention a four-month-old baby. Tanner could help. Tanner *would* help.

"You could stay with me when you come," she said. "It seems silly to pay for an empty apartment."

"Your place has one bedroom," he said. "So unless you plan on marryin' me, that's not gonna work."

She jerked in his arms like she'd been jolted with a dose of electricity. "You think we should get married?"

"I think that's what people do when they're in love." He chuckled. "We can go on a few more dates if you have a requirement for that."

She giggled and snuggled into him. "I love you."

"And I choose you," he said, pressing his lips to her temple. "I'd like to go to sleep now."

"All right, cowboy," she whispered. "You do that."
So he did.

CHAPTER FOURTEEN

The chirping of Summer's phone woke her. An intense heat next to her made her groan before she realized that heat came from Tanner. The man was a living, breathing furnace. She eased out of his arms without waking him and hurried over to her phone as it chimed again.

There are 41 medical facilities in Colorado Springs. The text from Belinda made Summer blink rapidly to make sure she'd read it correctly.

She started to type out a response when another text came in. *Margie Googled it. Just thought you might want to know.*

Summer erased her previous message and wrote, *Why would I need to know that?*

Because I'm sure some of them need a good nurse.

Her arms fell to her sides as if someone had tied bricks to her hands. Questions streamed through her mind:

When did Margie Google anything? How did Belinda come up with the wildest ideas that actually had merit? Could she really move to Colorado Springs?

The thought seemed ridiculous at first. She lived and worked in Three Rivers. She loved Three Rivers. Her parents were there. Her friends. Her job. Her life.

But her heart belonged to Tanner Wolf, and he couldn't go back to Three Rivers, at least not right now.

It wasn't a choice at all, really. She'd follow Tanner from here until the end of the Earth if it meant they could be together.

He groaned and she spun back to him. His eyes fluttered open as she moved to his side. "Hey, baby." She swept his hair off his forehead. "You awake? I want to talk to you about something."

He sat up and wiped the sleepiness from his face. "I think I'm awake. I feel like I've been run over." He exhaled and yawned. "What time is it?"

She checked her phone. "Almost nine o'clock."

"I told my mom I'd pick her up at ten and we'd go see how Bill was doing." He rubbed his eyes.

Summer nodded, a smile quickly dancing across her face. "Okay. Can we talk about me moving to Colorado Springs first? I can get a job here. There are forty-one health care facilities in this city."

He stared at her, those dark eyes drinking her in, considering her words. "You want to move to Colorado Springs?"

"It's better than you paying for an apartment you won't

live in." She shrugged like she didn't have anything to lose by leaving Three Rivers. "It's easier for me to move right now. I want to be with you."

He smiled, but it dimmed quickly. "It won't be forever. There's nothing for me to do here."

She glanced around his house, in awe of its magnificence. "You obviously don't need to work."

"Maybe not for the money," he admitted. "But I'm not one to just sit around all day."

"We can move every year if you want. Right now, you need to be here, and I need you."

He leaned forward and cupped her face in his hands. "I got really lucky that you were my nurse." He kissed her with desire, with heat, with love.

She giggled. "Yes, you sure did, cowboy."

ONE YEAR LATER:

"So take that box over there." Summer nodded toward a pile already in front of the hearth. Ethan moved in that direction, a dark look on his face. Tanner followed him, adding another box to the pile. She'd sold her house and moved to Colorado Springs, but it felt good—right—to be back in her hometown.

Tanner had come down himself, picked out the house she now stood in. It was around the corner from Brynn and Ethan's, built by the same general contractor, and it was the most beautiful house Summer had ever lived in. Well, the most beautiful house she'd live in after tomorrow's wedding.

"I can't believe y'all are movin' and gettin' married in the same week," Ethan said. "It's more excitement than Three Rivers has seen in a long time."

"Sure." Tanner slung his arm around Ethan's shoul-

ONE YEAR LATER:

ders. "And your baby's due when? Oh, that's right. On Friday."

Ethan grinned, a look of wonder on his face. Summer hoped Tanner would wear a look like that when he was about to become a father. "Brynn's already having contractions. He could be here any day now."

"Make 'im wait until after the wedding," Tanner said. "We get tomorrow. He can have any day after that."

"I'll talk to him," Ethan said dryly. "It's not like I asked you to move and get married at the same time my first son is being born."

"Ditto," Tanner shot back as the men moved out the front door. Summer smiled as she watched them go. It would be good for Tanner to be back in Three Rivers, back with Ethan, back on the ranch. He started his job there in just two weeks—immediately upon their return from their honeymoon.

Happiness sped through Summer at the thought of being Mrs. Tanner Wolf. The past year had been filled with challenges, but none of them seemed to be her own. She'd supported, she'd worked hard, and most of all, she'd prayed for patience. She'd needed it.

But now…now it was her turn to be in the spotlight. Her turn to be the bride. Her turn to start the life she'd always hoped she'd have.

"You ready for this?" Tanner's heated breath floated over the back of her neck, and she shivered.

"Totally ready." She turned into his arms and leaned in

for a fantastic kiss with her soon-to-be husband. "Are you?"

"Sweetheart, I've been ready to marry you since the day I met you."

Warmth spread from Summer's toes to the top of her head. "I'm glad we chose the thirteenth to get married. I don't care what anyone says about bad luck every seven years."

"Lucky number thirteen," he murmured just before kissing her in a way that testified of his love for her.

SNEAK PEEK! THE CURSE OF FEBRUARY FOURTEENTH
CHAPTER ONE

𝒞al Hodgkins dusted his palms together as he left the stables at Bowman's Breeds, located out at Three Rivers Ranch. He took a moment to enjoy the dusky light and perfect temperatures at this time of year. October was definitely the best month to be outside in Texas.

"You goin' to the dance tonight?" Garth Ahlstrom paused as he walked past, fully turning when Cal didn't answer right away. "There's dancing," the foreman of the ranch continued, a playful twinge in his tone. "Cookies. Costumes. Girls." A full-fledged smile galloped across his face with the last word.

Cal gave him an obligatory smile. He liked dancing, that was for sure. And cookies. He could do without the costumes, though he'd sent his six-year-old daughter a yellow princess dress so she could be appropriately dressed for her first grade Halloween party. Her mother and his ex-wife had sent pictures from the festivities earlier that day.

"Maybe," Cal said, thinking of his quiet cabin and the grilled cheese sandwich he could enjoy with a documentary about professional wrestling he'd found last weekend but hadn't had time to watch yet.

Garth, another silver-haired man like Cal, ducked his hat and continued on his way. Done with the horse care for the day, Cal strolled toward his cabin, his mind already wandering through the fields at the ranch he loved so much.

"You goin' to the dance?" Sawyer asked.

"Maybe," Cal told the cowhand.

Step, step, step.

"You goin' to the dance?" Beau asked.

"Maybe," Cal told his next-door neighbor.

He'd just reached his steps when Bennett stuck his head out of the barn doors. "A bunch of us are fixin' to go to the dance at seven-thirty." He grinned at Cal like they were old pals. Sure, Cal liked hanging out with the boys, but that was exactly the problem.

They were boys, none of them over thirty.

He was the only one who'd been married, the only one with a child who came to the ranch every other weekend, the only one who lived in a cowboy cabin alone.

"You're welcome to come." Bennett stepped out of the barn fully and leaned against the side of it.

"I don't—"

"Come on," Bennett said. "You can't stay cooped up

here all weekend. It's Halloween." He said it like Halloween was some great holiday, not to be missed.

Cal couldn't say he didn't fit with the other boys, wasn't interested in women, even though at thirty-nine-years-old he *didn't* fit and he *wasn't* interested in finding another mother for Sabrina.

But a companion for himself.... He sighed. "Seven-thirty?"

Bennett whooped and crossed the gravel path between the barns and the cabins. "You'll have fun, Cal."

"What are you dressing up as?"

"Cowboys." Bennett grinned and practically skipped back into the barn.

Cal couldn't help chuckling, and he had to admit that his heart took a bit of courage at not having to spend the evening alone. He usually liked being alone, but it had been a difficult week of work, dealing with a couple of pregnant horses on the ranch and then an accident at Brynn's that left two of her champion trainees hobbling around.

He hurried into his cabin and showered, putting on his best cowboy clothes, the ones he normally wore to church each Sunday. He got his grilled cheese and he managed to squeeze in a few minutes of that documentary before he headed through the barns to the parking lot. He didn't have to look far to find the boys heading into town.

The truck looked full already, with four men piled in the back. Their laughter rang through the clear air and almost made Cal turn around and go on home.

But Bennett had seen him, and he waved and said, "C'mon, Cal. We're gonna be late."

"It's seven-twenty-five," Cal said as he appraised the options for seating.

"Saved you a spot in the cab." Bennett grinned at him and leaned closer. "Had to convince Sawyer that the old man needed it." He laughed as he danced away from Cal's disdainful look. "Get in, Cal."

Cal got in. The forty-five minute drive into Three Rivers was filled with chatter between Bennett and his cabin mate, Beau. All the boys at the ranch called them B&B, because they never seemed to go anywhere without the other. As if their similarities weren't already enough, they were dating a set of sisters in town, who of course, would be at the dance tonight.

Cal listened to them talk about how they'd recognize the girls, as they were very excited about the prospect of a masked ball.

That got Cal's attention. "Masks?"

"All the women are wearing masks," Bennett said. "I just know I'm gonna fail at picking out Ruby."

"So I'm not even going to know who I'm dancing with?" Cal shifted on the seat.

"Nope."

Cal looked out the window, running through his options. He could go get ice cream at the shop down the street, wander the town until Bennett called and said it was time to go. He could—

"You're going," Bennett said. "I can practically see what you're thinkin'."

"What if I have to dance with Margaret?" Cal asked, not wanting to be rude, but, well, he simply couldn't do that again. Not that he'd ever danced with her, because the very idea sent a shudder through his muscles.

"Oh, Margaret," B&B said at the same time. They exchanged a glance, which didn't lift Cal's spirits at all.

"You guys gotta keep her away from me," Cal said.

"We've gotta—" Beau started at the same time Bennett said, "Sure, boss. Double wing men, at your service." He turned toward the downtown park, where the summer dances and other town festivals were always held. With three blocks still to go, the vehicles started thickening along the curbs.

Bennett pulled over into the next spot he saw and everyone piled out of the truck. Seven cowboys made quite the scene as they made their way to the party in full swing in the park. Cal automatically hung back while the other boys forged on, almost infected by the vibe in the country music staining the air.

Cal had fallen back three paces before Bennett turned to find him. "C'mon, boss," he called, and Cal wished he wouldn't call him "boss." He wasn't anyone's boss; it was just something Bennett called every man older than him.

Cal didn't come on. Something shook him inside. Probably all the bodies on the dance floor that had been laid over the grass. Or the dozens of people who wore masks. Any of them could be Margaret.

He lifted a red plastic cup of punch to his lips and drank the sugary-sweet liquid. Maybe he could just hang out here until he was sure Margaret wasn't here.

"C'mon." Bennett shouldered him, and Cal tried to twist away, only to find his second wingman there to block him. Together, B&B practically shoved him away from the refreshment tables.

"She's the one," Bennett said under his breath and pointed to a tall, lithe woman wearing a tight pair of black jeans, a tank top in the same shade, and a brilliant pair of orange monarch butterfly wings.

Her sun-kissed skin shone like the moon among all the black she wore—including a mask in the shape of butterfly's wings.

She definitely wasn't Margaret, and Cal found himself voluntarily walking toward her. He glanced right, expecting to see Bennett there to give him some advice, but Cal was very much on his own.

The butterfly wore a pair of black cowgirl boots with pale blue stitching in the shape of wings. She seemed hardly able to walk in the boots, but she continued toward him as if they were tethered together by some unknown line.

"Hey," Cal said when they were a few paces apart.

She didn't speak, but simply stared at him with blue-gray eyes behind the black mask.

A ballad came over the speakers. "You wanna dance?" Cal's voice seemed stuck in his throat, but sound managed to cross the space between them.

She nodded, and Cal extended his hand toward her. Her fingers were long, her skin tanned, her muscles defined. She stood only a few inches shorter than him, and she touched him with the grace and power of an athlete.

He wondered who she was, and when she'd come to town, as he'd never seen her before. And he liked to think he would've remembered. Of course, he didn't get to town much, other than church and the occasional grocery store run, but still. Talk of this woman would've made it through the cowboys in a matter of days.

Cal put one hand on her waist and she put one hand on his shoulders. They swayed, and Cal cursed himself for his slow tongue. But Butterfly didn't seem to have any problem with his lack of conversation, and she made no attempt to make small talk.

"Are you new in town?" he finally asked.

"Yes," she said. He could barely hear her, and he wanted to categorize the sound of her voice.

"What brings you to Three Rivers?"

"Not much." She lifted one sexy shoulder in a shrug.

Cal swallowed, wishing for that punch. He glanced around, trying to find a familiar face and being met with only blurred features and garish masks.

Butterfly stumbled in her too-big boots, and Cal steadied her. He tipped his head down, the brim of his hat nearly touching her forehead. Her wings bobbled, and a chuckle covered the awkwardness between them.

"You okay?" he asked.

"Just fine." She strengthened her grip on his shoulder,

and he didn't mind that one little bit. "What's your name?" she asked.

"Cal Hodgkins."

A quick smile passed her lips but it didn't even get close to her eyes. He watched her, sensing something turbulent had brought her to Three Rivers. He understood the feeling, the pull the town had to wounded souls. He'd come to Three Rivers after his divorce four years ago, thinking he'd just stay for the night, thinking he was just passing through.

Then he'd met Heidi Ackerman in her bakery, and the woman had found out he was a veterinarian, and that was that. Cal didn't know that at the time, but he could see it now. Could see God's hand in leading Cal to that bakery, on that day, at that time. Heidi was Squire's mother, and Squire owned the ranch that had given Cal a purpose in his life. In many ways, that quick stop at the bakery for breakfast had saved Cal's life.

The song ended, and Butterfly stepped out of his arms. Cal's hands fell to his sides, lifeless. A sense of complete emptiness filled him, for no reason he could understand.

She ducked her head and a lock of dark hair fell across her mask. She pushed it back and shot him the first smile he'd seen from her.

Her eye caught something over his shoulder and all happiness left her features. "I have to go," she said.

"Wait. What's your name?" Cal called after her, but the butterfly spun and hurried away. She stumbled, almost tripped, and continued. She reached the edge of the dance floor, the edge of the crowd. If she left the area, the darkness would swallow her in those dark clothes.

Cal hurried after her. "Wait," he tried again.

She glanced over her shoulder, and that was her undoing. She stepped onto the grass and down she went. Hard, too.

Cal shot forward, ready to help her up, help her back into his arms, where he wanted her to stay until he could get her name and phone number. But she was more agile than he'd given her credit for.

She leapt to her feet and took off into the darkness, leaving behind one black cowboy boot.

Cal reached the spot where she'd fallen, and he searched the darkness for a glimmer of her wings. "Wait," he said softly, to himself, before bending to pick up the winged cowgirl boot.

Second Chance Ranch: A Three Rivers Ranch Romance (Book 1): After his deployment, injured and discharged Major Squire Ackerman returns to Three Rivers Ranch, wanting to forgive Kelly for ignoring him a decade ago. He'd like to provide the stable life she needs, but with old wounds opening and a ranch on the brink of financial collapse, it will take patience and faith to make their second chance possible.

Third Time's the Charm: A Three Rivers Ranch Romance (Book 2): First Lieutenant Peter Marshall has a truckload of debt and no way to provide for a family, but Chelsea helps him see past all the obstacles, all the scars. With so many unknowns, can Pete and Chelsea develop the love, acceptance, and faith needed to find their happily ever after?

Fourth and Long: A Three Rivers Ranch Romance (Book 3): Commander Brett Murphy goes to Three Rivers Ranch to find some rest and relaxation with his Army buddies. Having his ex-wife show up with a seven-year-old she claims is his son is anything but the R&R he craves. Kate needs to make amends, and Brett needs to find forgiveness, but are they too late to find their happily ever after?

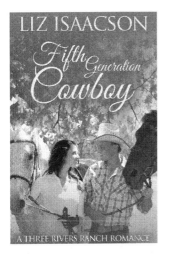

Fifth Generation Cowboy: A Three Rivers Ranch Romance (Book 4): Tom Lovell has watched his friends find their true happiness on Three Rivers Ranch, but everywhere he looks, he only sees friends. Rose Reyes has been bringing her daughter out to the ranch for equine therapy for months, but it doesn't seem to be working. Her challenges with Mari are just as frustrating as ever. Could Tom be exactly what Rose needs? Can he remove his friendship blinders and find love with someone who's been right in front of him all this time?

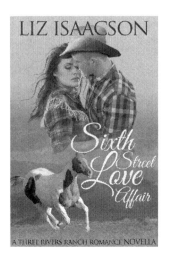

Sixth Street Love Affair: A Three Rivers Ranch Romance (Book 5): After losing his wife a few years back, Garth Ahlstrom thinks he's ready for a second chance at love. But Juliette Thompson has a secret that could destroy their budding relationship. Can they find the strength, patience, and faith to make things work?

The Seventh Sergeant: A Three Rivers Ranch Romance (Book 6): Life has finally started to settle down for Sergeant Reese Sanders after his devastating injury overseas. Discharged from the Army and now with a good job at Courage Reins, he's finally found happiness—until a horrific fall puts him right back where he was years ago: Injured and depressed. Carly Watters, Reese's new veteran care coordinator, dislikes small towns almost as much as she loathes cowboys. But she finds herself faced with both when she gets assigned to Reese's case. Do they have the humility and faith to make their relationship more than professional?

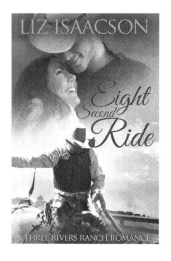

Eight Second Ride: A Three Rivers Ranch Romance (Book 7): Ethan Greene loves his work at Three Rivers Ranch, but he can't seem to find the right woman to settle down with. When sassy yet vulnerable Brynn Bowman shows up at the ranch to recruit him back to the rodeo circuit, he takes a different approach with the barrel racing champion. His patience and newfound faith pay off when a friendship--and more--starts with Brynn. But she wants out of the rodeo circuit right when Ethan wants to rejoin. Can they find the path God wants them to take and still stay together?

The First Lady of Three Rivers Ranch: A Three Rivers Ranch Romance (Book 8): Heidi Duffin has been dreaming about opening her own bakery since she was thirteen years old. She scrimped and saved for years to afford baking and pastry school in San Francisco. And now she only has one year left before she's a certified pastry chef. Frank Ackerman's father has recently retired, and he's taken over the largest cattle ranch in the Texas Panhandle. A horseman through and through, he's also nearing thirty-one and looking for someone to bring love and joy to a homestead that's been dominated by men for a decade. But when he convinces Heidi to come clean the cowboy cabins, she changes all that. But the siren's call of a bakery is still loud in Heidi's ears, even if she's also seeing a future with Frank. Can she rely on her faith in ways she's never had to before or will their relationship end when summer does?

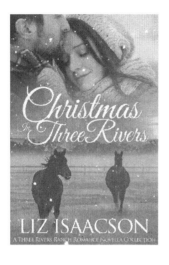

Christmas in Three Rivers: A Three Rivers Ranch Romance (Book 9): Isn't Christmas the best time to fall in love? The cowboys of Three Rivers Ranch think so. Join four of them as they journey toward their path to happily ever after in four, all-new novellas in the Amazon #1 Bestselling Three Rivers Ranch Romance series.

THE NINTH INNING: The Christmas season has never felt like such a burden to boutique owner Andrea Larsen. But with Mama gone and the holidays upon her, Andy finds herself wishing she hadn't been so quick to judge her former boyfriend, cowboy Lawrence Collins. Well, Lawrence hasn't forgotten about Andy either, and he devises a plan to get her out to the ranch so they can reconnect. Do they have the faith and humility to patch things up and start a new relationship?

TEN DAYS IN TOWN: Sandy Keller is tired of the dating scene in Three Rivers. Though she owns the pancake house, she's looking for a fresh start, which means an escape from the town where she grew up. When her older brother's best friend, Tad Jorgensen, comes to town for the holidays, it is a balm to his weary soul. A helicopter tour guide who experienced a near-death experience, he's looking to start over too--but in Three Rivers. Can Sandy and Tad navigate their troubles to find the path God wants them to take--and discover true love--in only ten days?

ELEVEN YEAR REUNION: Pastry chef extraordinaire, Grace Lewis has moved to Three Rivers to help Heidi Ackerman open a bakery in Three Rivers. Grace relishes the idea of starting over in a town where no one knows about her failed cupcakery. She doesn't expect to run into her old high school boyfriend, Jonathan Carver. A carpenter working at Three Rivers Ranch, Jon's in town against his will. But with Grace now on the scene, Jon's thinking life in Three Rivers is suddenly looking up. But with her focus on baking and his disdain for small towns, can they make their eleven year reunion stick?

THE TWELFTH TOWN: Newscaster Taryn Tucker has had enough of life on-screen. She's bounced from town to town before arriving in Three Rivers, completely alone and completely anonymous--just the way she now likes it. She takes a job cleaning at Three Rivers Ranch, hoping for a chance to figure out who she is and where God wants her. When she meets happy-go-lucky cowhand Kenny Stockton, she doesn't expect sparks to fly. Kenny's always been "the best friend" for his female friends, but the pull between him and Taryn can't be denied. Will they have the courage and faith necessary to make their opposite worlds mesh?

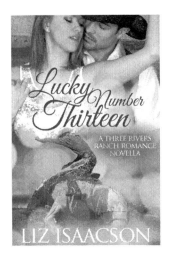

Lucky Number Thirteen: A Three Rivers Ranch Romance (Book 10): Tanner Wolf, a rodeo champion ten times over, is excited to be riding in Three Rivers for the first time since he left his philandering ways and found religion. Seeing his old friends Ethan and Brynn is therapuetic--until a terrible accident lands him in the hospital. With his rodeo career over, Tanner thinks maybe he'll stay in town--and it's not just because his nurse, Summer Hamblin, is the prettiest woman he's ever met. But Summer's the queen of first dates, and as she looks for a way to make a relationship with the transient rodeo star work Summer's not sure she has the fortitude to go on a second date. Can they find love among the tragedy?

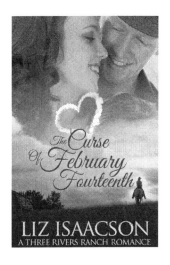

The Curse of February Fourteenth: A Three Rivers Ranch Romance (Book 11): Cal Hodgkins, cowboy veterinarian at Bowman's Breeds, isn't planning to meet anyone at the masked dance in small-town Three Rivers. He just wants to get his bachelor friends off his back and sit on the sidelines to drink his punch. But when he sees a woman dressed in gorgeous butterfly wings and cowgirl boots with blue stitching, he's smitten. Too bad she runs away from the dance before he can get her name, leaving only her boot behind...

Fifteen Minutes of Fame: A Three Rivers Ranch Romance (Book 12): Navy Richards is thirty-five years of tired—tired of dating the same men, working a demanding job, and getting her heart broken over and over again. Her aunt has always spoken highly of the matchmaker in Three Rivers, Texas, so she takes a six-month sabbatical from her high-stress job as a pediatric nurse, hops on a bus, and meets with the matchmaker. Then she meets Gavin Redd. He's handsome, he's hardworking, and he's a cowboy. But is he an Aquarius too? Navy's not making a move until she knows for sure…

Sixteen Steps to Fall in Love: A Three Rivers Ranch Romance (Book 13): A chance encounter at a dog park sheds new light on the tall, talented Boone that Nicole can't ignore. As they get to know each other better and start to dig into each other's past, Nicole is the one who wants to run. This time from her growing admiration and attachment to Boone. From her aging parents. From herself.

But Boone feels the attraction between them too, and he decides he's tired of running and ready to make Three Rivers his permanent home. **Can Boone and Nicole use their faith to overcome their differences and find a happily-ever-after together?**

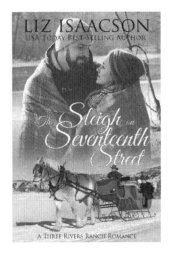

The Sleigh on Seventeenth Street: A Three Rivers Ranch Romance (Book 14): A cowboy with skills as an electrician tries a relationship with a down-on-her luck plumber. Can Dylan and Camila make water and electricity play nicely together this Christmas season? Or will they get shocked as they try to make their relationship work?

BOOKS IN THE CHRISTMAS IN CORAL CANYON ROMANCE SERIES

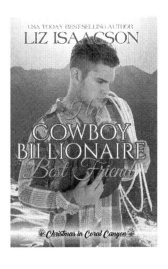

Her Cowboy Billionaire Best Friend (Book 1): Graham Whittaker returns to Coral Canyon a few days after Christmas—after the death of his father. He takes over the energy company his dad built from the ground up and buys a high-end lodge to live in—only a mile from the home of his once-best friend, Laney McAllister. They were best friends once, but Laney's always entertained feelings for him, and spending so much time with him while they make Christmas memories puts her heart in danger of getting broken again...

Her Cowboy Billionaire Boss (Book 2): Since the death of his wife a few years ago, Eli Whittaker has been running from one job to another, unable to find somewhere for him and his son to settle. Meg Palmer is Stockton's nanny, and she comes with her boss, Eli, to the lodge, her long-time crush on the man no different in Wyoming than it was on the beach. When she confesses her feelings for him and gets nothing in return, she's crushed, embarrassed, and unsure if she can stay in Coral Canyon for Christmas. Then Eli starts to show some feelings for her too...

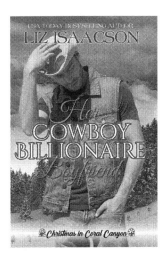

Her Cowboy Billionaire Boyfriend (Book 3): Andrew Whittaker is the public face for the Whittaker Brothers' family energy company, and with his older brother's robot about to be announced, he needs a press secretary to help him get everything ready and tour the state to make the announcements.

When he's hit by a protest sign being carried by the company's biggest opponent, Rebecca Collings, he learns with a few clicks that she has the background they need. He offers her the job of press secretary when she thought she was going to be arrested, and not only because the spark between them in so hot Andrew can't see straight.

Can Becca and Andrew work together and keep their relationship a secret? Or will hearts break in this classic romance retelling reminiscent of *Two Weeks Notice***?**

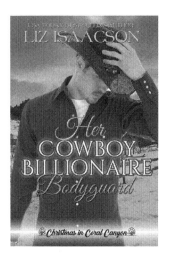

Her Cowboy Billionaire Bodyguard (Book 4): Beau Whittaker has watched his brothers find love one by one, but every attempt he's made has ended in disaster. Lily Everett has been in the spotlight since childhood and has half a dozen platinum records with her two sisters. She's taking a break from the brutal music industry and hiding out in Wyoming while her ex-husband continues to cause trouble for her. When she hears of Beau Whittaker and what he offers his clients, she wants to meet him. Beau is instantly attracted to Lily, but he tried a relationship with his last client that left a scar that still hasn't healed…

Can Lily use the spirit of Christmas to discover what matters most? Will Beau open his heart to the possibility of love with someone so different from him?

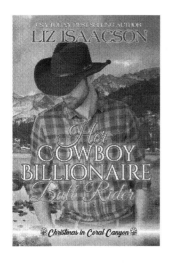

Her Cowboy Billionaire Bull Rider (Book 5): Todd Christopherson has just retired from the professional rodeo circuit and returned to his hometown of Coral Canyon. Problem is, he's got no family there anymore, no land, and no job. Not that he needs a job--he's got plenty of money from his illustrious career riding bulls.

Then Todd gets thrown during a routine horseback ride up the canyon, and his only support as he recovers physically is the beautiful Violet Everett. She's no nurse, but she does the best she can for the handsome cowboy. **Will she lose her heart to the billionaire bull rider? Can Todd trust that God led him to Coral Canyon...and Vi?**

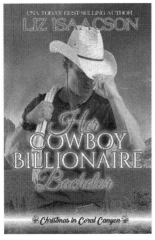

Her Cowboy Billionaire Bachelor (Book 6): Rose Everett isn't sure what to do with her life now that her country music career is on hold. After all, with both of her sisters in Coral Canyon, and one about to have a baby, they're not making albums anymore.

Liam Murphy has been working for Doctors Without Borders, but he's back in the US now, and looking to start a new clinic in Coral Canyon, where he spent his summers.

When Rose wins a date with Liam in a bachelor auction, their relationship blooms and grows quickly. **Can Liam and Rose find a solution to their problems that doesn't involve one of them leaving Coral Canyon with a broken heart?**

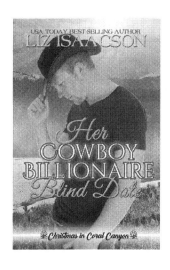

Her Cowboy Billionaire Blind Date (Book 7): Her sons want her to be happy, but she's too old to be set up on a blind date...isn't she?

Amanda Whittaker has been looking for a second chance at love since the death of her husband several years ago. Finley Barber is a cowboy in every sense of the word. Born and raised on a racehorse farm in Kentucky, he's since moved to Dog Valley and started his own breeding stable for champion horses. He hasn't dated in years, and everything about Amanda makes him nervous.

Will Amanda take the leap of faith required to be with Finn? Or will he become just another boyfriend who doesn't make the cut?

Her Cowboy Billionaire Best Man (Book 8): When Celia Abbott-Armstrong runs into a gorgeous cowboy at her best friend's wedding, she decides she's ready to start dating again.

But the cowboy is Zach Zuckerman, and the Zuckermans and Abbotts have been at war for generations.

Can Zach and Celia find a way to reconcile their family's differences so they can have a future together?

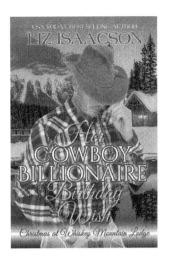

Her Cowboy Billionaire Birthday Wish (Book 9): All the maid at Whiskey Mountain Lodge wants for her birthday is a handsome cowboy billionaire. And Colton can make that wish come true—if only he hadn't escaped to Coral Canyon after being left at the altar...

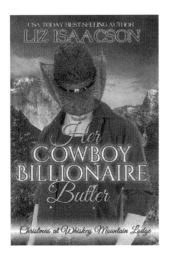

Her Cowboy Billionaire Butler (Book 10): She broke up with him to date another man...who broke her heart. He's a former CEO with nothing to do who can't get her out of his head. Can Wes and Bree find a way toward happily-ever-after at Whiskey Mountain Lodge?

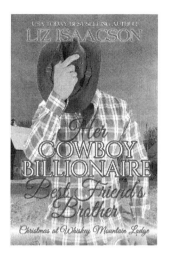

Her Cowboy Billionaire Best Friend's Brother (Book 11): She's best friends with the single dad cowboy's brother and has watched two friends find love with the sexy new cowboys in town. When Gray Hammond comes to Whiskey Mountain Lodge with his son, will Elise finally get her own happily-ever-after with one of the Hammond brothers?

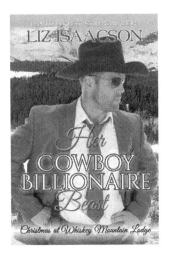

Her Cowboy Billionaire Beast (Book 12): A cowboy billionaire beast, his new manager, and the Christmas traditions that soften his heart and bring them together.

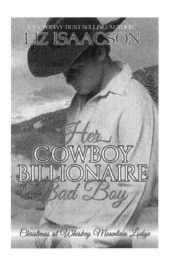

Her Cowboy Billionaire Bad Boy (Book 13): A cowboy billionaire cop who's a stickler for rules, the woman he pulls over when he's not even on duty, and the personal mandates he has to break to keep her in his life...

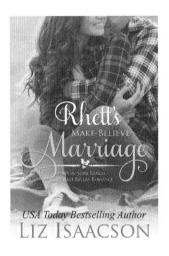

Rhett's Make-Believe Marriage (Book 1): She needs a husband to be credible as a matchmaker. He wants to help a neighbor. Will their fake marriage take them out of the friend zone?

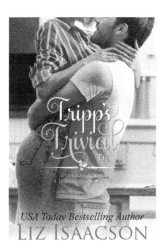

Tripp's Trivial Tie (Book 2): She needs a husband to keep her son. He's wanted to take their relationship to the next level, but she's always pushing him away. Will their trivial tie take them all the way to happily-ever-after?

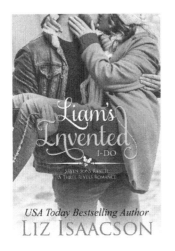

Liam's Invented I-Do (Book 3): She's desperate to save her ranch. He wants to help her any way he can. Will their invented I-Do open doors that have previously been closed and lead to a happily-ever-after for both of them?

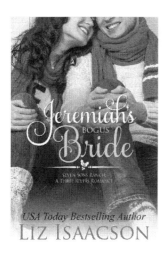

Jeremiah's Bogus Bride (Book 4): He wants to prove to his brothers that he's not broken. She just wants him. Will a fake marriage heal him or push her further away?

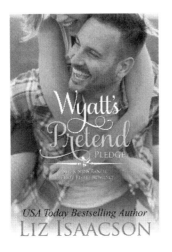

Wyatt's Pretend Pledge (Book 5): To get her inheritance, she needs a husband. He's wanted to fly with her for ages. Can their pretend pledge turn into something real?

Skyler's Wanna-Be Wife (Book 6): She needs a new last name to stay in school. He's willing to help a fellow student. Can this wanna-be wife show the playboy that some things should be taken seriously?

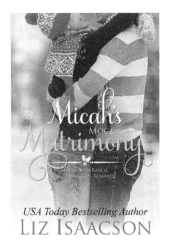

Micah's Mock Matrimony (Book 7): They were just actors auditioning for a play. The marriage was just for the audition – until a clerical error results in a legal marriage. Can these two ex-lovers negotiate this new ground between them and achieve new roles in each other's lives?

The Mechanics of Mistletoe (Book 1): Bear Glover can be a grizzly or a teddy, and he's always thought he'd be just fine working his generational family ranch and going back to the ancient homestead alone. But his crush on Samantha Benton won't go away. She's a genius with a wrench on Bear's tractors...and his heart. Can he tame his wild side and get the girl, or will he be left broken-hearted this Christmas season?

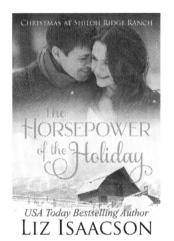

The Horsepower of the Holiday (Book 2): Ranger Glover has worked at Shiloh Ridge Ranch his entire life. The cowboys do everything from horseback there, but when he goes to town to trade in some trucks, somehow Oakley Hatch persuades him to take some ATVs back to the ranch. (Bear is NOT happy.)

She's a former race car driver who's got Ranger all revved up... Can he remember who he is and get Oakley to slow down enough to fall in love, or will there simply be too much horsepower in the holiday this year for a real relationship?

The Construction of Cheer (Book 3): Bishop Glover is the youngest brother, and he usually keeps his head down and gets the job done. When Montana Martin shows up at Shiloh Ridge Ranch looking for work, he finds himself inventing construction projects that need doing just to keep her coming around. (Again, Bear is NOT happy.) She wants to build her own construction firm, but she ends up carving a place for herself inside Bishop's heart. Can he convince her *he's* all she needs this Christmas season, or will her cheer rest solely on the success of her business?

The Secret of Santa (Book 4): Ace Glover loves to laugh, and everywhere he goes, luck seems to follow. When the hardworking cowboy volunteers to help with the Poinsettia Festival in town, he meets Sierra Broadbent. He's instantly smitten and loves spending time with her. She's in charge of the whole event, but she seems to disappear the moment everything starts...day after day.

When he learns her secret, the entire festival could be ruined—and so could Sierra's reputation and his new relationship with her. Will he keep his discovery to himself or will Sierra's secret become front-page news on Christmas Day?

BOOKS IN THE LAST CHANCE RANCH ROMANCE SERIES

Last Chance Ranch (Book 1): A cowgirl down on her luck hires a man who's good with horses and under the hood of a car. Can Hudson fine tune Scarlett's heart as they work together? Or will things backfire and make everything worse at Last Chance Ranch?

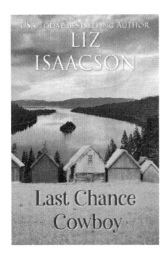

Last Chance Cowboy (Book 2): A billionaire cowboy without a home meets a woman who secretly makes food videos to pay her debts...Can Carson and Adele do more than fight in the kitchens at Last Chance Ranch?

Last Chance Wedding (Book 3): A female carpenter needs a husband just for a few days... Can Jeri and Sawyer navigate the minefield of a pretend marriage before their feelings become real?

Last Chance Reunion (Book 4): An Army cowboy, the woman he dated years ago, and their last chance at Last Chance Ranch... Can Dave and Sissy put aside hurt feelings and make their second chance romance work?

Last Chance Lake (Book 5): A former dairy farmer and the marketing director on the ranch have to work together to make the cow cuddling program a success. But can Karla let Cache into her life? Or will she keep all her secrets from him - and keep *him* a secret too?

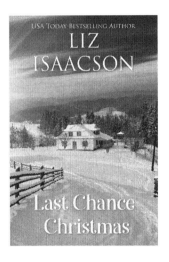

Last Chance Christmas (Book 6): She's tired of having her heart broken by cowboys. He waited too long to ask her out. Can Lance fix things quickly, or will Amber leave Last Chance Ranch before he can tell her how he feels?

BOOKS IN THE GRAPE SEED FALLS ROMANCE SERIES:

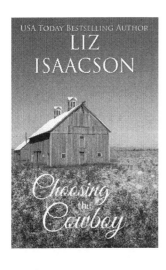

Choosing the Cowboy (Book 1): With financial trouble and personal issues around every corner, can Maggie Duffin and Chase Carver rely on their faith to find their happily-ever-after?

A spinoff from the #1 best-selling Three Rivers Ranch Romance novels, also by USA Today bestselling author Liz Isaacson.

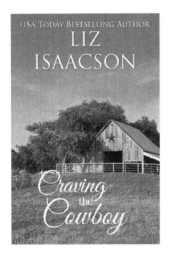

Craving the Cowboy (Book 2): Dwayne Carver is set to inherit his family's ranch in the heart of Texas Hill Country, and in order to keep up with his ranch duties and fulfill his dreams of owning a horse farm, he hires top trainer Felicity Lightburne. They get along great, and she can envision herself on this new farm—at least until her mother falls ill and she has to return to help her. Can Dwayne and Felicity work through their differences to find their happily-ever-after?

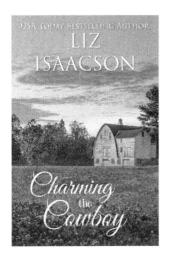

Charming the Cowboy (Book 3): Third grade teacher Heather Carver has had her eye on Levi Rhodes for a couple of years now, but he seems to be blind to her attempts to charm him. When she breaks her arm while on his horse ranch, Heather infiltrates Levi's life in ways he's never thought of, and his strict anti-female stance slips. Will Heather heal his emotional scars and he care for her physical ones so they can have a real relationship?

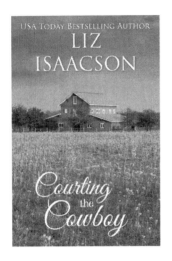**Courting the Cowboy (Book 4):** Frustrated with the cowboy-only dating scene in Grape Seed Falls, May Sotheby joins TexasFaithful.com, hoping to find her soul mate without having to relocate--or deal with cowboy hats and boots. She has no idea that Kurt Pemberton, foreman at Grape Seed Ranch, is the man she starts communicating with... Will May be able to follow her heart and get Kurt to forgive her so they can be together?

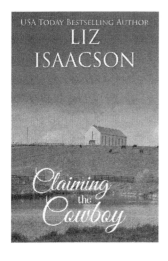

Claiming the Cowboy, Royal Brothers Book 1 (Grape Seed Falls Romance Book 5): Unwilling to be tied down, farrier Robin Cook has managed to pack her entire life into a two-hundred-and-eighty square-foot house, and that includes her Yorkie. Cowboy and co-foreman, Shane Royal has had his heart set on Robin for three years, even though she flat-out turned him down the last time he asked her to dinner. But she's back at Grape Seed Ranch for five weeks as she works her horse-shoeing magic, and he's still interested, despite a bitter life lesson that left a bad taste for marriage in his mouth.

Robin's interested in him too. But can she find room for Shane in her tiny house--and can he take a chance on her with his tired heart?

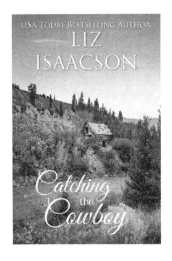

Catching the Cowboy, Royal Brothers Book 2 (Grape Seed Falls Romance Book 6): Dylan Royal is good at two things: whistling and caring for cattle. When his cows are being attacked by an unknown wild animal, he calls Texas Parks & Wildlife for help. He wasn't expecting a beautiful mammologist to show up, all flirty and fun and everything Dylan didn't know he wanted in his life.

Hazel Brewster has gone on more first dates than anyone in Grape Seed Falls, and she thinks maybe Dylan deserves a second... Can they find their way through wild animals, huge life changes, and their emotional pasts to find their forever future?

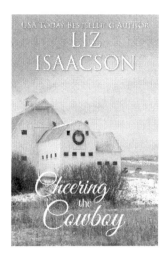

Cheering the Cowboy, Royal Brothers Book 3 (Grape Seed Falls Romance Book 7): Austin Royal loves his life on his new ranch with his brothers. But he doesn't love that Shayleigh Hatch came with the property, nor that he has to take the blame for the fact that he now owns her childhood ranch. They rarely have a conversation that doesn't leave him furious and frustrated--and yet he's still attracted to Shay in a strange, new way.

Shay inexplicably likes him too, which utterly confuses and angers her. As they work to make this Christmas the best the Triple Towers Ranch has ever seen, can they also navigate through their rocky relationship to smoother waters?

BOOKS IN THE STEEPLE RIDGE
ROMANCE SERIES:

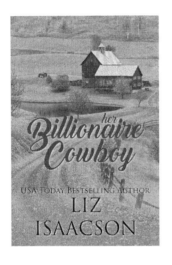

Her Billionaire Cowboy (Book 1): Tucker Jenkins has had enough of tall buildings, traffic, and has traded in his technology firm in New York City for Steeple Ridge Horse Farm in rural Vermont. Missy Marino has worked at the farm since she was a teen, and she's always dreamed of owning it. But her ex-husband left her with a truckload of debt, making her fantasies of owning the farm unfulfilled. Tucker didn't come to the country to find a new wife, but he supposes a woman could help him start over in Steeple Ridge. Will Tucker and Missy be able to navigate the shaky ground between them to find a new beginning?

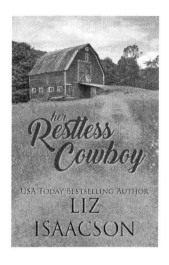

Her Restless Cowboy: A Butters Brothers Novel, Steeple Ridge Romance (Book 2): Ben Buttars is the youngest of the four Buttars brothers who come to Steeple Ridge Farm, and he finally feels like he's landed somewhere he can make a life for himself. Reagan Cantwell is a decade older than Ben and the recreational direction for the town of Island Park. Though Ben is young, he knows what he wants—and that's Rae. Can she figure out how to put what matters most in her life—family and faith—above her job before she loses Ben?

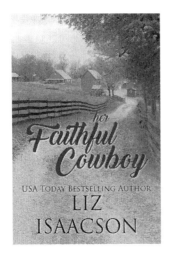

Her Faithful Cowboy: A Butters Brothers Novel, Steeple Ridge Romance (Book 3): Sam Buttars has spent the last decade making sure he and his brothers stay together. They've been at Steeple Ridge for a while now, but with the youngest married and happy, the siren's call to return to his parents' farm in Wyoming is loud in Sam's ears. He'd just go if it weren't for beautiful Bonnie Sherman, who roped his heart the first time he saw her. Do Sam and Bonnie have the faith to find comfort in each other instead of in the people who've already passed?

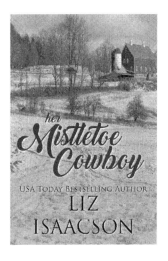

Her Mistletoe Cowboy: A Butters Brothers Novel, Steeple Ridge Romance (Book 4): Logan Buttars has always been good-natured and happy-go-lucky. After watching two of his brothers settle down, he recognizes a void in his life he didn't know about. Veterinarian Layla Guyman has appreciated Logan's friendship and easy way with animals when he comes into the clinic to get the service dogs. But with his future at Steeple Ridge in the balance, she's not sure a relationship with him is worth the risk. Can she rely on her faith and employ patience to tame Logan's wild heart?

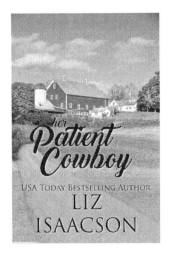

Her Patient Cowboy: A Butters Brothers Novel, Steeple Ridge Romance (Book 5): Darren Buttars is cool, collected, and quiet—and utterly devastated when his girlfriend of nine months, Farrah Irvine, breaks up with him because he wanted her to ride her horse in a parade. But Farrah doesn't ride anymore, a fact she made very clear to Darren. She returned to her childhood home with so much baggage, she doesn't know where to start with the unpacking. Darren's the only Buttars brother who isn't married, and he wants to make Island Park his permanent home—with Farrah. Can they find their way through the heartache to achieve a happily-ever-after together?

BOOKS IN THE HORSESHOE HOME RANCH ROMANCE SERIES:

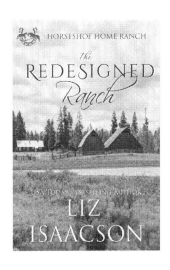

The Redesigned Ranch (Book 1): Jace Lovell only has one thing left after his fiancé abandons him at the altar: his job at Horseshoe Home Ranch. Belle Edmunds is back in Gold Valley and she's desperate to build a portfolio that she can use to start her own firm in Montana. Jace isn't anywhere near forgiving his fiancé, and he's not sure he's ready for a new relationship with someone as fiery and beautiful as Belle. Can she employ her patience while he figures out how to forgive so they can find their own brand of happily-ever-after?

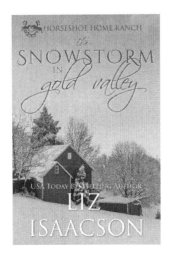

The Snowstorm in Gold Valley (Book 2): Professional snowboarder Sterling Maughan has sequestered himself in his family's cabin in the exclusive mountain community above Gold Valley, Montana after a devastating fall that ended his career. Norah Watson cleans Sterling's cabin and the more time they spend together, the more Sterling is interested in all things Norah. As his body heals, so does his faith. Will Norah be able to trust Sterling so they can have a chance at true love?

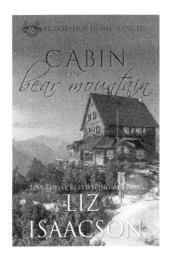

The Cabin on Bear Mountain (Book 3): Landon Edmunds has been a cowboy his whole life. An accident five years ago ended his successful rodeo career, and now he's looking to start a horse ranch--and he's looking outside of Montana. Which would be great if God hadn't brought Megan Palmer back to Gold Valley right when Landon is looking to leave. Megan and Landon work together well, and as sparks fly, she's sure God brought her back to Gold Valley so she could find her happily ever after. Through serious discussion and prayer, can Landon and Megan find their future together?

Be sure to check out the spinoff series, the Brush Creek Brides romances after you read FALLING FOR HIS BEST FRIEND. Start with A WEDDING FOR THE WIDOWER.

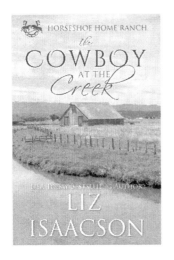

The Cowboy at the Creek (Book 4): Twelve years ago, Owen Carr left Gold Valley—and his long-time girlfriend—in favor of a country music career in Nashville. Married and divorced, Natalie teaches ballet at the dance studio in Gold Valley, but she never auditioned for the professional company the way she dreamed of doing. With Owen back, she realizes all the opportunities she missed out on when he left all those years ago—including a future with him. Can they mend broken bridges in order to have a second chance at love?

The Wedding in the Winter (Book 5): Caleb Chamberlain has spent the last five years recovering from a horrible breakup, his alcoholism that stemmed from it, and the car accident that left him hospitalized. He's finally on the right track in his life—until Holly Gray, his twin brother's ex-fiance mistakes him for Nathan. Holly's back in Gold Valley to get the required veterinarian hours to apply for her graduate program. When the herd at Horseshoe Home comes down with pneumonia, Caleb and Holly are forced to work together in close quarters. Holly's over Nathan, but she hasn't forgiven him—or the woman she believes broke up their relationship. Can Caleb and Holly navigate such a rough past to find their happily-ever-after?

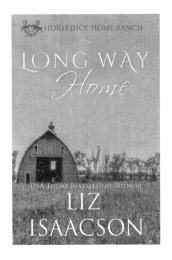

The Long Way Home (Book 6): Ty Barker has been dancing through the last thirty years of his life--and he's suddenly realized he's alone. River Lee Whitely is back in Gold Valley with her two little girls after a divorce that's left deep scars. She has a job at Silver Creek that requires her to be able to ride a horse, and she nearly tramples Ty at her first lesson. That's just fine by him, because River Lee is the girl Ty has never gotten over. Ty realizes River Lee needs time to settle into her new job, her new home, her new life as a single parent, but going slow has never been his style. But for River Lee, can Ty take the necessary steps to keep her in his life?

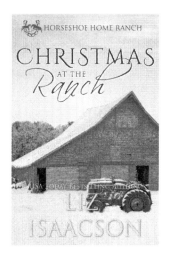

Christmas at the Ranch (Book 7): Archer Bailey has already lost one job to Emersyn Enders, so he deliberately doesn't tell her about the cowhand job up at Horseshoe Home Ranch. Emery's temporary job is ending, but her obligations to her physically disabled sister aren't. As Archer and Emery work together, its clear that the sparks flying between them aren't all from their friendly competition over a job. Will Emery and Archer be able to navigate the ranch, their close quarters, and their individual circumstances to find love this holiday season?

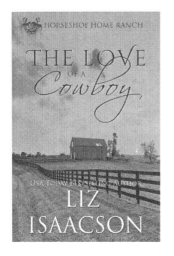

The Love of a Cowboy (Book 8): Cowboy Elliott Hawthorne has just lost his best friend and cabin mate to the worst thing imaginable—marriage. When his brother calls about an accident with their father, Elliott rushes down to Gold Valley from the ranch only to be met with the most beautiful woman he's ever seen. His father's new physical therapist, London Marsh, likes the handsome face and gentle spirit she sees in Elliott too. Can Elliott and London navigate difficult family situations to find a happily-ever-after?

BOOKS IN THE BRUSH CREEK BRIDES ROMANCE SERIES:

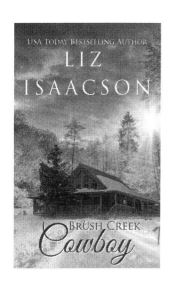

Brush Creek Cowboy: Brush Creek Cowboys Romance (Book 1): Former rodeo champion and cowboy Walker Thompson trains horses at Brush Creek Horse Ranch, where he lives a simple life in his cabin with his ten-year-old son. A widower of six years, he's worked with Tess Wagner, a widow who came to Brush Creek to escape the turmoil of her life to give her seven-year-old son a slower pace of life. But Tess's breast cancer is back...

Walker will have to decide if he'd rather spend even a short time with Tess than not have her in his life at all. Tess wants to feel God's love and power, but can she discover and accept God's will in order to find her happy ending?

The Cowboy's Challenge: Brush Creek Brides Romance (Book 2): Cowboy and professional roper Justin Jackman has found solitude at Brush Creek Horse Ranch, preferring his time with the animals he trains over dating. With two failed engagements in his past, he's not really interested in getting his heart stomped on again. But when flirty and fun Renee  Martin picks him up at a church ice cream bar--on a bet, no less--he finds himself more than just a little interested. His Gen-X attitudes are attractive to her; her Millennial behaviors drive him nuts. Can Justin look past their differences and take a chance on another engagement?

A Cowboy Proposal: Brush Creek Brides Romance (Book 3): Ted Caldwell has been a retired bronc rider for years, and he thought he was perfectly happy training horses to buck at Brush Creek Ranch. He was wrong. When he meets April Nox, who comes to the ranch to hide her pregnancy from all her friends back in Jackson Hole, Ted realizes he has a huge family-shaped hole in his life. April is embarrassed, heartbroken, and trying to find her extinguished faith. She's never ridden a horse and wants nothing to do with a cowboy ever again. Can Ted and April create a family of happiness and love from a tragedy?

A New Family for the Cowboy: Brush Creek Brides Romance (Book 4): Blake Gibbons oversees all the agriculture at Brush Creek Horse Ranch, sometimes moonlighting as a general contractor. When he meets Erin Shields, new in town, at her aunt's bakery, he's instantly smitten. Erin moved to Brush Creek after a divorce that left her 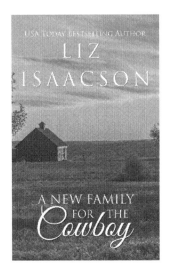 penniless, homeless, and a single mother of three children under age eight. She's nowhere near ready to start dating again, but the longer Blake hangs around the bakery, the more she starts to like him. Can Blake and Erin find a way to blend their lifestyles and become a family?

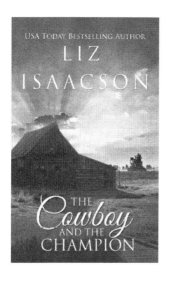

The Cowboy and the Champion: Brush Creek Brides Romance (Book 5): Emmett Graves has always had a positive outlook on life. He adores training horses to become barrel racing champions during the day and cuddling with his cat at night. Fresh off her professional rodeo retirement, Molly Brady comes to Brush Creek Horse Ranch as Emmett's protege. He's not thrilled, and she's allergic to cats. Oh, and she'd like to stay cowboy-free, thank you very much. But Emmett's about as cowboy as they come.... Can Emmett and Molly work together without falling in love?

Schooled by the Cowboy: Brush Creek Brides Romance (Book 6): Grant Ford spends his days training cattle—when he's not camped out at the elementary school hoping to catch a glimpse of his ex-girlfriend. When principal Shannon Sharpe confronts him and asks him to stay away from the school, the spark between them is instant and hot. Shannon's expecting a transfer very soon, but she also needs a summer outdoor coordinator—and Grant fits the bill. Just because he's handsome and everything Shannon's ever wanted in a cowboy husband means nothing. Will Grant and Shannon be able to survive the summer or will the Utah heat be too much for them to handle?

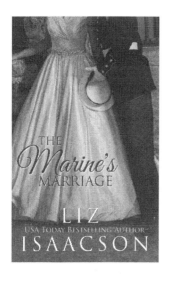

The Marine's Marriage: A Fuller Family Novel - Brush Creek Brides Romance (Book 1): Tate Benson can't believe he's come to Nowhere, Utah, to fix up a house that hasn't been inhabited in years. But he has. Because he's retired from the Marines and looking to start a life as a police officer in small-town Brush Creek. Wren Fuller has her hands full most days running her family's company. When Tate calls and demands a maid for that morning, she decides to have the calls forwarded to her cell and go help him out. She didn't know he was moving in next door, and she's completely unprepared for his handsomeness, his kind heart, and his wounded soul. Can Tate and Wren weather a relationship when they're also next-door neighbors?

The Firefighter's Fiancé: A Fuller Family Novel - Brush Creek Brides Romance (Book 2): Cora Wesley comes to Brush Creek, hoping to get some in-the-wild firefighting training as she prepares to put in her application to be a hotshot. When she meets Brennan Fuller, the spark between them is hot and instant. As they get to know 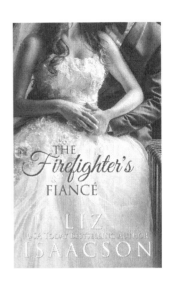 each other, her deadline is constantly looming over them, and Brennan starts to wonder if he can break ranks in the family business. He's okay mowing lawns and hanging out with his brothers, but he dreams of being able to go to college and become a landscape architect, but he's just not sure it can be done. Will Cora and Brennan be able to endure their trials to find true love?

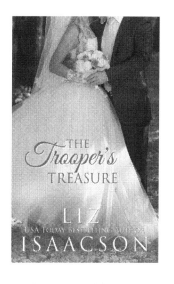

The Trooper's Treasure: A Fuller Family Novel - Brush Creek Brides Romance (Book 3): Dawn Fuller has made some mistakes in her life, and she's not proud of the way McDermott Boyd found her off the road one day last year. She's spent a hard year wrestling with her choices and trying to fix them, glad for McDermott's acceptance and friendship. He lost his wife years ago, done his best with his daughter, and now he's ready to move on. Can McDermott help Dawn find a way past her former mistakes and down a path that leads to love, family, and happiness?

The Detective's Date: A Fuller Family Novel - Brush Creek Brides Romance (Book 4): Dahlia Reid is one of the best detectives Brush Creek and the surrounding towns has ever had. She's given up on the idea of marriage—and pleasing her mother—and has dedicated herself fully to her job. Which is great, since one of the most perplexing cases of her career 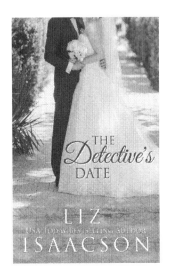 has come to town. Kyler Fuller thinks he's finally ready to move past the woman who ghosted him years ago. He's cut his hair, and he's ready to start dating. Too bad every woman he's been out with is about as interesting as a lamppost—until Dahlia. He finds her beautiful, her quick wit a breath of fresh air, and her intelligence sexy. Can Kyler and Dahlia use their faith to find a way through the obstacles threatening to keep them apart?

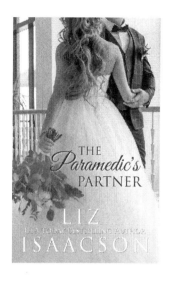

The Paramedic's Partner: A Fuller Family Novel - Brush Creek Brides Romance (Book 5): Jazzy Fuller has always been overshadowed by her prettier, more popular twin, Fabiana. Fabi meets paramedic Max Robinson at the park and sets a date with him only to come down with the flu. So she convinces Jazzy to cut her hair and take her place on the date. And the spark between Jazzy and Max is hot and instant...if only he knew she wasn't her sister, Fabi.

Max drives the ambulance for the town of Brush Creek with is partner Ed Moon, and neither of them have been all that lucky in love. Until Max suggests to who he thinks is Fabi that they should double with Ed and Jazzy. They do, and Fabi is smitten with the steady, strong Ed Moon. As each twin falls further and further in love with their respective paramedic, it becomes obvious they'll need to come clean about the switcheroo sooner rather than later...or risk losing their hearts.

The Chief's Catch: A Fuller Family Novel - Brush Creek Brides Romance (Book 6): Berlin Fuller has struck out with the dating scene in Brush Creek more times than she cares to admit. When she makes a deal with her friends that they can choose the next man she goes out with, she didn't dream they'd pick surly Cole Fairbanks, the new Chief of Police.

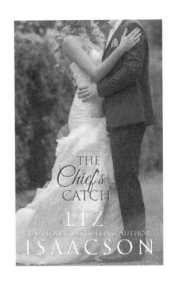

His friends call him the Beast and challenge him to complete ten dates that summer or give up his bonus check. When Berlin approaches him, stuttering about the deal with her friends and claiming they don't actually have to go out, he's intrigued. As the summer passes, Cole finds himself burning both ends of the candle to keep up with his job and his new relationship. When he unleashes the Beast one time too many, Berlin will have to decide if she can tame him or if she should walk away.

ABOUT LIZ

Liz Isaacson writes inspirational romance, usually set in Texas, or Montana, or anywhere else horses and cowboys exist. She lives in Utah, where she walks her dogs daily, watches a lot of Netflix, and eats a lot of peanut butter M&Ms while writing. Find her on her website at lizisaacson.com.

Made in the USA
Columbia, SC
12 October 2021